CREATURES OF THE NIGHT

There was a leathery swish of wings, then a giant bat, with a seven-foot wingspread, hovered in the light from the broken ceiling.

"A carrion bat!" Alon shouted, seizing Sheela's arm and pulling her toward the stairs. The room was filled with the beat of wings as the monstrous creature swooped after them. Alon jerked Sheela to the dusty marble floor, narrowly avoiding the sharp claws on the bat's grasping, elongated fingers as it swept past above them. They were on their feet and running, while the bat circled the large room, which resounded with its shrill cries and flapping wings. As they reached the stairs, the thing was upon them....

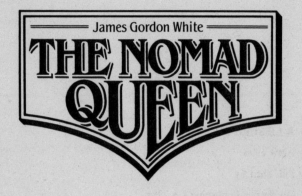

James Gordon White

THE NOMAD QUEEN

LEISURE BOOKS   **NEW YORK CITY**

*To my wife Marie
for her unwavering
love, belief and
support through our
years together*

A LEISURE BOOK®

April 1993

Published by

Dorchester Publishing Co., Inc.
276 Fifth Avenue
New York, NY 10001

Printed in the United States of America.

Chapter One

A blood-red moon bathed the corpse-littered battlefield in its pale, ghastly light. There in the broad forest clearing, from dawn till dusk, over three thousand Thorgon barbarians had thrown themselves against the mighty army of Imperial Rhobia, and almost fought them to a standstill. But raw courage and an eagerness to defend their homeland, in fair and noble combat, had not been enough against seasoned, highly disciplined troops skilled in the civilized arts of war. The Thorgons had died as hard as they fought, and well over twice their number of Rhobian campaigners had bled their last for the glory of their mad emperor.

Now, after five years of steady encroachment, the Rhobian army had finally succeeded in clearing the way for their conquest of the Northern Forest lands, and there was celebrating that night. But for many, no amount of heady wine or ale could dull the memory of those towering, half-naked, pale-blond barbarians and their fierce women screaming in blood-lust as they broke the invincible Rhobian square and spread a two-handed death with sword and battle axe.

Only the overwhelming weight of sheer numbers and the stout determination to stand and fight, backed by the knowledge that the reserve archers and cavalry would slay all who fled, had carried the day for the campaigners. The Thorgons were vanquished, but the mention of their name would forever strike fear in the hearts of Rhobians.

While the campaigners huddled around their fires, the campfollowers, laden with sacks of plunder, moved like ghoulish specters among the dead. The Thorgons, who were known to adorn themselves before battle with golden objects as talismans, were especially prized, and knife rule prevailed in that contested area of the battlefield.

Old Jugarus grinned crookedly as the wounded Thorgon youth's eyes changed from defiance to fear at the touch of his knife. He savored the moment. No longer was he a limping object of ridicule tagging behind the marching army, eating their dust with the hordes of whores and other parasites, his advice ignored by the new breed of campaigners; he was once again a man to be feared. With practiced skill he drew the blade across the barbarian's neck. Then he sat back laughing as a high red geyser erupted from the ragged wound and splattered upon his madly writhing victim's brawny bare chest. The youth's glazed eyes reflected pain and horror, and Jugarus was pleased that he, too, had witnessed the grisly sight.

Voices were heard arguing nearby. Jugarus looked back and saw a man and two women tugging at a corpse like curs struggling for possession of a bone. Hastily he stripped the gold ornaments from his kill and hobbled on, dragging his heavy sack, determined to keep ahead of the others who were slowly closing in to challenge his territorial claim.

Skirting a dead horse, Jugarus came upon a tall Thorgon girl lying in the midst of over half a dozen dead campaigners.

By the gods, here had been a wench to be reckoned with!

The old campaigner reconstructed the battle in his mind as his eyes slowly swept over the area. She had been unhorsed, after riding down a campaigner and impaling a second with her lance, during an impetuous charge that left her separated from her group. The barbarians' instinct to fight as individuals rather than as a unit was always their undoing. With sword and knife she had slain all who came at her. And even when her weapons were broken she had managed to dispatch still another with her jagged sword before she was felled—probably by a slingman's lead pellet, as no arrows or gaping wounds were visible.

The girl's heavy, ornate gold necklace glittered in the moonlight, but caution bridled the old man's greed. As a forty-year veteran of barbarian campaigns, he was well aware that these wenches sometimes played at death to entice their prey. His bloody knife held ready, Jugarus sidled forward pulling his sack after him. He ignored the campaigners, whose purses rarely contained enough to purchase a cup of wine, and went straight to the girl.

Cautiously he knelt beside her and brushed the matted bloodstained hair back from her face, noting with surprise that her cheek was still warm to his touch. He chuckled hoarsely and nodded as he saw the mass of clotted blood above her hairline, which partly hid the ugly round wound, and the dried red stream that coursed down the side of her face and neck and narrowed to a thin line between her breasts. It was the work of a sling-man's pellet; he had seen that wound often enough. Curious, he turned her head to better see her face, and the sight caused him to suck air between his broken yellow teeth.

She had the startling beauty of a goddess!

As Jugarus continued staring all thoughts of loot momentarily vanished. Her features were exquisite, with high proud cheekbones, sculptured nose, delicate red lips and long silken lashes, closed as if in sleep. Her face was framed by a flowing mane of white-gold hair that caught and softly reflected the moonlight. He sat back on his heels and let his eyes roam down her graceful neck and straight shoulders to her magnificent golden body.

A brief strip of soft white leather with crisscrossing thongs in front did little to conceal the firm, boldly pointed breasts. Her stomach was smooth and flat, her waist slender, and the matching strip of leather with crisscrossing thongs on each side left her narrow hips almost bare. The long shapely legs disappeared below the knees into snug-fitting boots of the same soft white leather, and their high thin heels reminded Jugarus of the ones worn by the Amazons to the far South.

He forced his eyes from the girl and laughed aloud as he cast a sweeping glance at the surrounding campaigners. He had no wish to detract from the wench's valor, but the fools had probably made her task easier by letting their eyes stray from her weapons; a common but deadly mistake often made by these young campaigners who had never seen, much less fought an Amazon. A woman was a much more cunning and savage enemy than any man; brawn was of little advantage, and the slightest display of chivalry meant death.

Turning back to the girl, he muttered a thanks to the combined deities of Rhobia that she had not been mutilated in battle. Even in death she fired his loins as no live woman had over the long years since his youth. It mattered naught that she was a corpse; alive she would respond no better. A barbarian wench fought like a she-demon until she was tied down. And still she had to be gagged, and her hair bound to a stake, otherwise, she would smash a man's nose with her forehead and open his face or neck with her teeth. Once she was totally secured and the man was on top, she went limp and no threat or punishment could make her respond. Jugarus grinned self-consciously and rubbed a gnarled hand over his flattened nose as dim memories stirred in a shadowy corner of his mind.

The sound of a struggle, closely followed by a wounded yelp, reminded him that the looters were now close at hand, and would soon pass him by, usurping his claim to what bodies lay ahead. Jugarus fretted over the unjust dilemma bestowed by the fickle gods. Reason urged him to strip the wench of her gold and begone. But passion urged him to tarry while she was still warm and supple. Unlike the temple harlots she would accept his unbridled lust without protest or refusal, and would not look upon him with scorn afterwards. Besides, how much gold did an old man need; his sack was nigh filled, and there would be other battles.

Jugarus made his decision and lurched to his feet. Drawing his time-bent frame erect and brandishing his knife and a huge fist for emphasis, he bellowed in his best old campaigner's voice for all to stay clear of his patch of ground or come to a bloody end.

A chorus of ragged voices replied with derisive taunts, several casting dire suppositions as to his lineage, but no scavenger intruded. Jugarus stood watching the small bands sullenly skulk past, veering wide of his area. Then, with excited cries, they scurried toward a strewn pile of hacked and gory corpses, cursing, shoving, tripping one another in their haste to reach the spoils first. He paid them little heed; let the greedy swine kill themselves over what pickings lay ahead.

Protectively drawing his sack to him, Jugarus knelt beside the girl. For all too short a while she would help him forget the hard lot that fate and the gods had decreed. It was no blessing for an old campaigner to live too long. Better to have died during the prime of life in glorious combat, surrounded by comrades who would morn his passing and speak well of him before his funeral pyre, than to outlive the ability to ply one's only trade in a world of uncaring strangers.

Almost tenderly, he turned the bloody side of the girl's face away from him. She had not lost a trace of her warmth. That was good. He could take her at his leisure. Jugarus jabbed his knife into the ground on the other side of her, so that he could grab it and the sack in either hand if a poacher intervened. His calloused hands caressed her still form as he slowly lowered his once-mighty bulk onto her. Luxuriating in the feel of her soft young body, he half closed his eyes and let his mind drift.

He was again that youthful campaigner of long ago; a bull of a man, admired by his comrades, feared by his enemies, and irresistible to the wenches. The wench was a captive Amazon who had been buffeted nigh unconscious. He would tame her in front of his comrades and, to their disbelief and envy, have the man-hater begging to be his willing slave.

Was it an illusion, or did the wench actually stir beneath him?

Lost in dreams of youth, Jugarus was undisturbed—until the wench's head turned. He watched in a strange, dreamlike fascination as her eyelids flew open and two large amber orbs stared into his, blank and uncomprehending. Then a flame of intelligence flashed in those eyes, and with it came recognition, fear, and a fierce hatred of an enemy. The glowing eyes penetrated his brain, shattering any uncertainty of reality.

So startling was the intensity of her hatred that his superstitious mind was certain this was the wench's avenging spirit, returned by the barbarians' Great Earth Mother Goddess to punish him for the sacrilege he intended to her corpse.

She was moving!

He felt the strength surging through her limbs and a blind panic paralyzed his mind. He forgot all else, but that he should flee—now!

As Jugarus shoved himself to his knees, something flashed in the moonlight. It was cold and sharp, and it brought great pain as it ripped across his throat. He sagged back on his heels, suddenly feeling weak, and stared in curious wonder at the red fountain that burst forth before his eyes, splattering upon the wench's bare belly and legs as she scooted away. He saw the horror and revulsion on her face, and recognized the thing that glinted in her hand—it was his own knife! His hands went to his neck, felt the warm life's blood streaming between his fingers.

The wench had slit his throat!

With that realization came a clarity of thought, and he would have laughed aloud, had not his vocal cords been severed. The wench had been alive all the while. He had allowed himself to be taken in just like a raw recruit. How these new campaigners would laugh when told of how wise old Jugarus had met his end. The moon must have dipped behind the clouds, as darkness was about him. Jugarus' mind struggled to find some comfort from the thought that the gods, in their irony, had benevolently allowed him to die upon the battlefield.

Then the blackness engulfed him and he thought no more.

The tall Thorgon girl stood staring down with large frightened and confused eyes at the hulking dead man grotesquely kneeling before her with bowed head, as she had oft seen her people pay homage to her father upon his raised throne within his mead hall. She was dimly aware of the sticky warmth of his blood oozing down her body, and his bloody knife clutched in her hand. Wrenching her eyes away, she frantically sought to orient herself while her dazed mind strove to compose her thoughts.

The fierce pain in her head brought back the memory of a Rhobian sling-man standing off at a cowardly distance and unleashing his sling at the moment she had lunged and driven her shattered sword into the face of a charging soldier who was about to swing his short double-edged sword. As the man's face had dissolved into red ruin, there had been a blinding flash inside her skull, accompanied by a pain such as she had never known, and then darkness.

But the Great Earth Mother had not yet called her to her bosom. Upon waking she had seen an ugly bearlike face leering down at her, and had felt a great bulk threatening to crush the life from her slim body. Recognizing an enemy, she had reacted out of a barbarian's self-preservation instinct; and she spared no remorse for the lifeless object squatting at her feet.

A sudden shout startled her from her thoughts. She whirled and saw a group of ill-clad men cautiously shambling toward her through the carnage. Pillagers of the dead. They were far worse than any Rhobian campaigner. She must avoid capture at all cost. Her eyes swept the expanse of tangled, skewered corpses to the dark forest looming beyond. If she could reach its shelter none would dare follow.

There were more shouts, and she saw other tattered bands rising up from among the dead like carrion crows. The nearest bunch was parting, seeking to encircle her.

Unmindful of the scattered corpses, the tall girl dashed with feral grace across the blood-drenched field toward the safety of the dense forest.

Stimulated by the prospect of a chase, excited howls went up from the groups as they bolted after her like hungry wolves in pursuit of a wounded doe.

Ahead, the girl saw a brutish figure running to intercept her.

She veered.

So did he.

They closed rapidly.

Suddenly a corpse shifted violently beneath her foot. She stumbled, flinging her hands out to break the fall, and landed on hands and knees. Before she could stand the man was upon her. His hand roughly caught her hair and yanked her upright on her knees. The girl looked up at the cruelly grinning face and the raised club poised to strike. Instinctively she slashed out at the protruding belly. The blade sank in, marking its path with a long red line.

The man's hands dropped to his wound as he staggered back, screaming. He tripped against a corpse and sat down heavily on its armored chest, his legs sprawled before him. Ignoring the fleeing girl, he stared stupidly at his entrails as they slithered forth, snakelike, from his bloody stomach. Then he became violently ill.

The sight of the dying man had a sobering effect upon his fellow pursuers, and most of them immediately abandoned the chase to return to their safe occupation. After all, where was the sport when the prey was armed and deadly?

Aided by the moon disappearing behind the clouds, the girl reached the forest and plunged into the safety of its dark dominion. She pressed against a tree and stood gasping deep lungfuls of air while looking back for her pursuers.

The men stopped at the forest's perimeter and milled about hurling futile taunts and curses, but none were brave enough to do more.

Her trials now ended, the tall girl turned and, moving with pantherish stealth, went in search of her father and her people.

The faint sound of wagon bells told her that she was near the clearing where the High Priestess and her virgins had waited, along with the women who were unable to take part in the battle. As the High Priestess prayed to the gods, the women stood ready to kill those who cowardly retreated from the field of battle.

That they were still there meant the place was a rallying point for her people. She would find her father and three brothers plotting strategy, while the High Priestess made augury for the morrow's battle, and the women gave aid and encouragement to the warriors.

She saw her father as he had looked before entering battle: his long white hair and fierce mustache stiff with lime and bristling like a horse's mane, his iron jaw and battle scarred face solemn, yet his gray eyes gleamed with the prospect of taking the field against a long hated enemy. Time and again he had sent the Rhobians scurrying back to their border like frightened rats. On their previous invasion, he had personally taken the head of a Rhobian consul and, after embalming it in cedar oil, proudly displayed it in a gilded chest. Many new Rhobian heads would be added to his chest, of that she was certain.

She smiled, imagining her father's consternation on seeing her bathed with the blood of their enemies; she must look more dead than alive. As in her childhood when she came running to him after rough play with her older brothers, he would probably glower, then melt with love and concern and soothe her ails with gentle words and embraces. Though she had taken part in previous skirmishes, she was now returning from her first major battle, and her tales of valor would wring hearty praise from her father and three brothers.

Lost in contemplation, the girl was almost to the clearing before her intuitive instincts suddenly warned her that something was amiss. She stood listening, straining all of her senses. The only sounds ahead were the wagon bells and the flapping of cloth in the wind. Gripping her knife, she cautiously crept forward on feet that only a creature of the wild would detect.

Even before she saw it, the girl sensed the aura of death that hung over the clearing. From the shadows she stared in stunned horror at the sight before her.

The moonlit clearing was filled with the bodies of Thorgon men and women. Those strewn in contortions of grim agony had obviously fled from battle, but most lay grouped in orderly rows about the High Priestess' large six-wheeled wagon that dominated the clearing. They had died willingly—but why?

The girl tried to find logic in the senseless act. Surely her father and brothers were not among these sacrificial sheep? Though she had seen and smelt enough of death this day, she must know. Steeling herself, the tall girl hesitantly entered the clearing and began her grisly task.

The wind stirred the wagon's felt canopy. Its small brass bells lent a macabre contrast to the sepulchral sounds of the wind and the banners flapping from the supporting poles. Bent over a corpse, the girl suddenly froze at the sound of a feeble voice, barely audible above the wind, calling her name. Her eyes shifted over the rows of dead, but none moved. She strained to hear above the wind. Then, as she was about to accuse her overwrought senses of jesting with her, the voice came again.

"Sheela! Come to me, my princess!"

The girl recognized the voice and turned toward the wagon. The High Priestess sat propped against its middle wheel. Her white robe was mostly crimson; the sacrificial knife buried in her side, up to its golden hilt, added her own blood to that of the sacrifices. Weakly she extended an elaborately tattooed arm and beckoned her hither.

Weaving her way through the maze of corpses, the tall girl hastened to the older woman and knelt beside her. The High Priestess' face had a deathly pallor beneath her cryptic tattoos, which stood out in bright contrast, and a thin stream of blood ran down one corner of her mouth. Her dark eyes were glazed with pain and delirium, but a spark of vitality still glowed. Her bloody hand clasped the girl's forearm, drawing her nearer.

"I have been here dying since the moon rose," she said, her voice thick with blood.

21

Her face contorted into the ghastly semblance of a smile as her eyes focused on the girl. "But I now understand why the Great Earth Mother ignored my pleas for release. My task is yet undone."

Sheela cared little about the woman's task. She had never been very fond of the High Priestess and held many religious doubts, which her father had cautioned her against expressing publicly. Oft was the time he had reminded her that, regardless of his own convictions, a king must respect his people's beliefs, or soon lose his throne. She knew the old woman had little time, and she must learn the fate of her family. Setting down her knife, she leaned closer.

"I would know of my father and brothers?" she asked, trying to keep the urgency from her voice.

"King Heathgan and his sons fell in honorable combat. You, my princess, are now queen—and the last living Thorgon."

It was the answer she had secretly known and feared. The words pierced her brain like a sword of ice, chilling and numbing all thought. She wanted to speak, cry, express some emotion, but icy talonlike fingers clutched her throat in a paralyzing grip. So she sat motionless, a beautiful frozen statue, devoid of all feeling or emotion. The High Priestess was speaking, but her words fell upon deaf ears.

Very slowly she became aware of the woman's long clawlike nails digging into her forearm, drawing blood. Though the pain was minimal, it told Sheela that she was still capable of some feeling, and roused her from her trancelike state. A white-hot flame coursed through her veins, melting her icy grief and restoring animation to her limbs. She savagely jerked her arm free from the woman's grasp and glared at her accusingly as her fury mounted.

"Bitch!" she spat. "Your augury of triumph was false—as are you and your harsh gods!" She made a contemptuous sweeping gesture up at the flapping banners with their totem beast emblems.

Fierce indignation flared in the dying woman's eyes as she retorted, her voice stronger, full of self-righteousness, "My prophecies were true. We Thorgons have again triumphed over the Rhobian invaders."

"My father and brothers dead. Our people scattered about us like sacrificial animals— if that be triumph, I'll have none of it!"

The tattooed woman's face abruptly softened. Then she said, as if to a child, "Do not blaspheme in your grief, Sheela. Know you not that there is but a momentary break between life and death when we pass from this world into the otherworld? Our people freely chose death and salvation. They have triumphed by escaping Rhobian slavery for the freedom of the otherworld."

Sheela stared at her incredulously. This foul hag had convinced her superstitious people to do exactly what the enemy sought to accomplish. A land without its people; so much the better for their scheme. Now their own people could settle it without fear of bloody raids of reprisal, and the Rhobian empire had gained new undisputed boundaries. Were this priestess of death and betrayal not already a living corpse, Sheela would gladly give the sacrificial knife a strong twist and hasten her departure to the laps of her beloved gods. But that would be a charitable act; and Queen Sheela, last of the Thorgons, felt no charity in her heart for her sole subject. The woman's suffering was small recompense for the enormity of her crimes, but Sheela wished her to linger on as long as her austere gods would allow.

The High Priestess spoke, but a strong gust of wind flapped the wagon's canopy and banners loudly, obscuring her words.

With a painful effort, she leaned toward the girl and caught her wrist for support.

"The time is near," she gasped, her face and eyes glowing with delirium and strange ecstasy. "Your father and people anxiously await our arrival in the otherworld."

Sheela shook her head savagely. "No, old woman, you journey alone. I'll not quit this life a coward!"

Had Sheela not been so intent upon her defiance, she would have seen the High Priestess' other hand pick up her own knife and slowly raise it. Oblivious, she continued to vent her long pent-up rage upon the woman who had intimidated her since childhood, and now robbed her of her people.

"Your otherworld may be as false as you. Instead of a continuation of life, you may find only a black void where your spirit will wander alone—deaf, dumb, and sightless—for eternity." She waved a hand in dismissal. "I bid you take your leave of me and discover which of us speaks truthfully!"

Her face alight with an insane rage, the High Priestess plunged the knife down at the unsuspecting girl's bare back.

But a thick staff suddenly deflected the blade scant inches from its goal.

Thwarted in her final effort, the tattooed woman fell back with a hideous dying shriek of inhuman fury.

The startled girl turned and saw a gaunt, bent figure in a black hooded robe looming over her with a raised staff. She shrank back, instantly raising one arm to ward off the expected blow. But instead the figure lowered the long staff to the ground and leaned heavily upon it with both hands.

"I mean you no harm, my queen," said a rich, kindly voice full of warmth and compassion.

Sheela frowned, confused. She did not recognize the voice, yet there was something familiar about the figure. A pale hand brushed back the hood, and she stared up at a nigh bone-white face, with sharp, wrinkled features and shoulder-length gray hair streaked with black. She gasped involuntarily as she recognized old Tokar the crookback; a tribal outcast not only because of his deformity, which should have condemned him at birth, but for his disdain of their harsh gods, and rumors that he was a witch-man. His abrupt, yet timely appearance hinted at sorcery.

Tokar smiled at her surprise and, moving forward, said in polite rebuke, "You really should have been more cautious. Ethelda was never one to taunt." He stopped and addressed the tattooed corpse. "Were you, most sacred High Priestess?" He prodded it with his staff, as if expecting a reply. Had the corpse seen fit to sit up and converse, Sheela would have quitted the clearing on winged feet. Then Tokar turned and regarded her with his penetrating deep blue eyes.

Uncomfortable under his gaze, Sheela managed a wan smile to conceal her apprehension. "I am in your debt, Tokar."

The old man nodded. "I am most pleased to accept your gratitude, my queen." He waved a hand down at the dead woman. "Your defiance of Ethelda's will places you in high stead. Perhaps there is yet hope for the Thorgon nation."

"If you heard our conversation, then surely you know that I am a queen without subjects," Sheela said bitterly.

"Our enemy won this day, but his conquest is far from assured. The High Priestess lied. Many escaped the battle with their lives."

She asked skeptically, "Know you that as fact?"

The shaggy gray head nodded in affirmation. "There are those who would fight other battles, rather than throw their lives away in one futile contest. They are now scattered

27

throughout this forest."

"I must hasten to them!" she said heartened, springing to her feet. The swift movement brought a sudden rush of dizziness; she swayed unsteadily, her head throbbing most painfully. A strong pale hand caught her arm and steadied her.

"Later, my queen," Tokar said soothingly. "Now you must accept my humble hospitality."

Sheela tensed, remembering chilling childhood tales of what befell those foolish enough to enter the cave of this witch-man. Was his kindness merely a ruse to lure her there and wreak vengeance upon the last of the royal Thorgons for the hurt that had been done him over the years? Still, she must not reveal to him that a queen could know fear.

Summoning a smile that she hoped would pass for sincerity, she said, "I fear I am unable to accept your generosity, Tokar. I must rally my people for the morrow's opposition."

"Aye, my queen, but you must not present yourself to them looking as one freshly arisen from the grave. They have suffered a most demoralizing defeat this day. You must display yourself hale and hardy, brimming with confidence—every inch a proud queen."

She could not fault his logic. A skillful show would be required. Though with both mind and body fast succumbing to the day's ordeal, she gravely doubted her ability to break her people's mood of defeat. But were Tokar's words spoken from true concern, or did they mask a sinister motive?

A gust of cold wind whipped across the clearing bringing the surrounding stench of death, and loudly snapping the banners and clanging the canopy's bells. The violent combination of sound and smell overwhelmed Sheela's sorely strained senses. Her eyes teared involuntarily as the throbbing in her skull was magnified a hundredfold. She gagged, resisting the impulse to yield to the wave of nausea that swept her insides. Her slender form trembled with a sudden chill. She clenched her teeth against it and the nausea, while trying to focus her blurred vision upon Tokar's face as his words came to her across a seeming abyss.

"My cave is not far. Come, my queen, you are greatly in need of rest. There is naught here but death. Let us tarry no longer."

Sheela sought to protest, but the swooning pain befuddled her mind. She was too weak to resist as Tokar gently but firmly drew her from the clearing.

The journey was a nightmarish blur of monstrous shapes and images in Sheela's delirium-tortured brain. Her bleeding wound felt afire, pounding incessantly with each faltering step she took. Her limbs ached with fatigue as her superb body, driven far beyond its endurance, rapidly gave way to numbness. Again and again she stumbled, but Tokar's firm hand retained its grip on her arm and guided her onward. How long they continued she knew not.

Then they were before a yawning maw in the middle of a towering rock face, with Stygian darkness stretching beyond. Though pain and exhaustion had almost driven all consciousness from her, Sheela was aware of a primitive fear urging her not to enter as Tokar bore her toward the black opening. With a cry of desperation she twisted free of his grasp and reeled away. Swaying on ungainly limbs, she shook her head and defiantly glared at the witch-man.

Sharply contrasted by the black hood, Tokar's pale face shone like a death skull in the moonlight. His indistinct words came to her from afar as he approached, hand outstretched.

Sheela willed herself to turn and run, but her flight was cerebral. Her strength was spent. The skeletal face before her spun dizzily in a dark vortex. Then her legs buckled beneath her and she fell headlong into the enveloping vertiginous blackness.

Chapter Two

But the blackness was not eternal.

Very slowly a gray luminesence crept through the darkness, and Sheela found herself in a gloomy, mist-covered clearing ringed by silent ghostly sentinels of imposing gray megaliths, streaked with age. A chorus of sepulchral voices called her name. Through the swirling mist she caught a fleeting glimpse of four men.

Her father and brothers!

Joyfully shouting their names, she ran toward them. But the dense fog smothered her calls and obscured her vision. Blindly she stumbled forward clawing at the thick clouds, seeking to penetrate their dankness, which clung to her like a shroud.

Abruptly the fog lifted, and she stood before the smiling figures of her father and brothers. Arms outstretched, she went to embrace her father. But upon her touch, his body became a decaying corpse and crumbled in her grasp. Sheela shrank back, her eyes wide with horror and disbelief; a scream lodged in her throat. She turned to her brothers, only to see their rotting remains scattered about her.

A woman's derisive laughter echoed through the clearing.

Sheela whirled and saw the High Priestess standing between two of the towering gray rocks.

"There, my foolish queen, is your family of this world," she said contemptuously. "Now look you upon the otherworld which you so arrogantly rejected!" She stepped aside and motioned out into the surrounding blackness.

Sheela gasped in awe as a golden light, of a brillance far greater than the spectrum of Earth's natural sunlight, revealed a radiant land of unsurpassed beauty. There, amid waving foliage and warm sunshine, her father, brothers, and other Thorgons went about their lives in serene bliss.

"Cherish this sight long in your memory, Sheela," spoke the High Priestess, "for you will never again see this world. Your blasphemies have condemned your soul to wander through an eternity of darkness." She made the mockery of a bow. "Farewell, Queen Sheela, last of the Thorgons in this world!" Then she turned and walked into the bright land, and the light slowly began to dim after she had entered.

Giving an anguished cry, Sheela bolted forward as the light continued to wane and the swirling mist returned. She reached the megaliths, only to find her way barred by an invisible veil. Frantically she threw herself against it as the vision on the other side faded to darkness.

But the veil was unyielding.

Overcome by remorse and aloneness, Sheela fell to her knees and sobbed wildly. Suddenly her arm was seized in a bone-crushing grip. She uttered a startled cry and raised her head, wincing at the pain.

Old Tokar's pale face glared into hers as he hissed venomously, "Come, my good queen, your reward awaits you!"

Her eyes followed his sweeping gesture to a sinister gray stone altar in the middle of the misty clearing. She recoiled, but the strong pale hand held her firmly.

"Nay, as the last royal Thorgon you cannot

escape your destiny," he sneered, yanking her to her feet and dragging her forward into the dense fog . . .

Sheela lay naked, spread-eagled on her back, her wrists and ankles firmly lashed with thongs to the corners of the altar. The rough cold stone chilled her body, as did the fog which formed damp droplets on her bare skin. The witch-man stood beside her, his face ghastly in the moonlight.

"For well over three score years I have patiently suffered the stigma of my deformity from a people who vainly place more importance upon a perfect body than what lies within one's heart and mind." His eyes glowed with malice. "Is it not just that upon your death, I, Tokar, the despised crookback, will be the last of the proud, godlike Thorgons!"

She trembled at his dreadful laughter. He bent closer as the whisps of fog sought to separate them, and she felt his warm rancid breath upon her face.

"You shall die slowly, delicately," he whispered, as if sharing an intimate secret. "I will increase your pain a little at a time, but you will never lose consciousness or sink into delirium until I have wrung the final exquisite agony from your flayed body."

He stepped back, reached into his robe and withdrew a long gleaming knife with strange cryptic symbols engraved upon it. His face was a mask of pure evil as he slowly raised the knife high.

Her amber eyes large and pleading, Sheela twisted vainly in her tight bonds. A scream of utter hopelessness and terror rose from deep within her. But before it could pass her quivering lips, a dense billowing cloud of fog encompassed her and seemed to fill her mouth . . .

Something soft and thick was wadded inside her mouth.

Sheela bit down, felt a hard center between the muffling folds. She tried to dislodge it, but her tongue was depressed and her jaw could scarcely move. Something else was thrust against the soft corners of her mouth. She felt a tight indentation along her cheeks, and there was a pressure at the back of her neck. Confused, she opened her eyes and stared up at a lofty, uneven rock ceiling.

She was inside Tokar's cave!

Quickly she sought to sit up, but her body would not respond. An attempt to raise her head was to no avail and made her aware of a confining band around her forehead.

Her wound still throbbed painfully, and she felt her warm blood trickling down the side of her face, contrasting the chill of her damp body. Lowering her eyes from the dark ceiling, she saw a stick with thongs attached at either end protruding from the sides of her mouth. Then she noticed that her breasts were bare and glimmered with moisture. She shifted her eyes to one side and tensed.

A large burnished silver bowl and a wet bloodstained cloth were on a small rudely built table. Her reflection in the bowl explained her distress.

She was securely bound to a narrow hide-covered bench. Her body had been washed clean of blood, and she still wore her boots and the strip of leather about her hips. Ropes fastened her wrists and ankles to the legs on either side of the bench. Several lengths of rope wound about her waist, chest, and forehead holding her flat against the bench. A stick, wrapped in the middle with a heavy cloth, was wedged between her teeth. Her hair, she noted curiously, was tautly drawn back from her face, tied in a bunch at the top of her head with a thong, and draped in sweeping piles over the end of the bench to the floor below.

Sheela stared in strange fascination at her reflection. Before she had been dreaming—but this was no dream. Her premonition had come true. She was Tokar's captive. And, indeed, he intended to take his revenge.

When would he come to her? What terrible agonies did he have planned? Would she be able to bear them bravely? To die in battle was noble; but to be slowly tortured to death. . . . She shuddered as, against her will, her imagination unleashed a myriad of vivid, horrifying images.

Then she heard a noise.

Sheela lay rigid with expectation. Desperately she sought the source of the sound out of the corner of her eye. It was the witch-man. She caught a glance of his black robe and pale face before he moved out of her line of vision. Quickly she closed her eyes, feigned sleep. Her wildly pounding heartbeat threatened to deafen her ears to his shambling steps and the heavy tap of his staff as he approached. Never had she known fear as she did now.

Nearer he came.

Fighting back her rising panic, Sheela surreptitiously exerted the full strength of her magnificent body against the imprisoning ropes. Impossible. She was pinned immobile to the bench.

He was almost to her.

She lay still, silent. Very cautiously she parted her eyelids. Her long silken lashes distorted her vision, adding an eerie tangle to the dark shadows upon the high rock ceiling. He was at the bench now. He stood over her, out of her vision. She heard his labored breathing, heard the staff placed on the floor. She waited, nerves taut as bowstrings. What cruelty would he first inflict upon her naked, helpless body?

Slowly his pale face loomed over her. She was surprised that he expressed no fiendish glee but appeared to be gravely scrutinizing her. His fingers lightly brushed a few strands of hair away from her wound, and she squeezed her eyes shut, wincing inwardly at his touch to the sensitive area. Had she not been so securely gagged, she would surely have betrayed herself by crying out. After an eon, the hand moved away but did not leave her. She felt it firmly grip her hair where it had been tied together with the thong. Then she became aware of an intense heat above her. Again, she parted her eyelids and looked out through her lashes. What she saw filled her with ultimate horror.

A glowing knife was descending toward her head.

As she felt the scorching heat almost upon her flesh, she suddenly understood the witchman's intent—it was even more diabolical that she had imagined. Like all Thorgons, he believed that the head housed the soul. He was about to open her head and take her soul! The High Priestess had been right—never would she enter the otherworld; her soul was condemned to an eternity of darkness and suffering.

In another instant, the iron-red blade would be upon her.

Sheela's eyes sprung open and a mewling cry escaped her gag as she frantically heaved against her bonds, oblivious to the hurt she did to her slender body.

And then the searing knife touched her scalp.

A meteoric flash burst before her eyes. A fiery pain burned into her brain. An anguished, soul-emptying scream tore through her gag as her teeth violently clamped down on the wadding, snapping the stick. Her pain-maddened body arched convulsively against its restraints, and the sturdy bench trembled beneath her. Mind and body screamed in unison for release.

And the dreaded blackness mercifully took her.

There was the delicious aroma of boiling stew and baking bread.

Sheela was curiously aware that she was very hungry. But how could that be unless . . . Forgetting all caution, she quickly opened her eyes. Tokar stood staring down at her. She gasped and shrank away.

"Fear not, my queen," he said soothingly, "you are safe from all harm."

Sheela abruptly realized that she was no longer bound and looked down at herself. She lay on an elevated sleeping platform, with several blankets covering her and a large soft pillow beneath her head. Her clothing and necklace were on a nearby bench. Bewildered, she glanced about at her surroundings. In the middle of the large room was a rock lined fire-pit over which a kettle of stew hung between two poles. Bread was baking in a brick oven on the far side of the room. Torches were set at intervals throughout the room, and gaily colored tapestries decorated the walls. There was naught to hint at menace. The room was as cheerful and cozy as her own lodgings. Had it all been the dream of a mind addled by delirium? But the pain had been too real, too intense. Her hand went to her head; a cloth covered her wound.

"Careful," Tokar said, "do not disturb the poultice. Its healing task is not yet completed." He sat on a stool beside the bed, set the staff across his lap, and smiled. "How does Your Highness feel this day?"

"Most refreshed," she replied, rather startled that, indeed, it was true.

The old man nodded, pleased. "My herbs and potions have done well by you." Then he added modestly, "But I must not detract from the power of sleep. You have lain abed six nights now."

Sheela sat up with a start and ignored her modesty as the blankets fell about her waist. "I have lost that long?"

Tokar placed a restraining hand on her shoulder. "It could not be helped. Your wound was most grievous."

"What of my people—and the Rhobians?"

"Our people," Tokar politely emphasized, "are gathering into small resistance bands to harry the enemy, who still licks his wounds and strays not far from camp."

Sheela drew the blankets about her breasts and leaned back on one elbow. Then, carefully choosing her words, she said, "Tokar, I recall vague memories of lying bound whilst you applied a heated knife to my scalp." She eyed him evenly. "Was it naught but a dream?"

He shook his shaggy head and met her eyes directly. "I acted from necessity, not malice. The bleeding refused to cease. Had I not cauterized the wound, you would surely have died."

"I am badly scarred?" she asked hesitantly, fearing his reply.

"No, my queen," he answered reassuringly. "I am well versed in the healing arts. I give you my solemn oath that there is no disfigurement."

Sheela felt a flood of relief. She was greatly aware of her exceptional beauty, and her pride was almost narcissistic. Though she had gladly endangered it in battles for her homeland, there was always the trust that she would never be marred.

"Again, I thank you, Tokar. I stand many times in your debt."

" 'Tis naught," he replied, unsuccessfully attempting to conceal his own gratitude at her words. He leaned closer. "Your father once aided me. Now I am greatly pleased to be of service to his daughter."

"How did he aid you?"

"The High Priestess desired to roast me in one of her wicker baskets, but King

Heathgan would have none of it."

Sheela remembered the hideous sight of the gigantic wickerwork artifacts, filled with shrieking victims, illuminating the night sky with flames. Though such offerings were made only in time of a dire crisis and the sacrifices were criminals and prisoners of war, they had always repelled her. Once she had accompanied her father and brothers to such a sacrifice, and afterwards no amount of threats or cajoling could make her return. Still, at those times, it had been impossible to completely shut out the distant sounds of screams and chants, even though she avoided looking toward the blazing beacons on the sacred hill.

"I am both pleased and surprised to learn that my father ever denied the High Priestess. What induced him to do so?"

"It was done out of reverence to your mother's memory."

Sheela was completely taken aback. "My mother . . ."

Tokar nodded. "She championed me whilst she lived, though she was unable to change my status as outcast."

Sheela had been little more than a child when her mother died, but the memory was still painful. She thought of a tall, graceful woman of extreme beauty, with a gentle manner and music in her voice. She could easily imagine her mother taking up the cause of a poor unfortunate such as Tokar.

Tokar waved a pale hand about at the walls. "Many tapestries and other niceties you see were gifts from her." He smiled in fond remembrance. "Though I would insist that her visits alone brought ample joy, still she ofttimes came with gifts to brighten up my 'palace,' as she used to call it." He studied her thoughtfully. "You have much of her appearance. It is almost as if she is again visiting."

Sheela smiled at the compliment while inwardly chiding herself for her previous fear and distrust and, worst of all, neglect of this man her mother had befriended. Then she guiltily averted her eyes and said, "It must be most lonely for you."

He shrugged. "I have long ago grown accustomed to it."

Still she detected a trace of sadness in his voice, and asked, "How do you pass your time?"

"It is filled with uncovering the mysteries of the mind. That knowledge compensates me greatly."

"Yet if there is none to share that knowledge with . . ." She broke off, becoming acutely aware of her own loneliness. Now well past her twentieth summer, she had since resigned herself to the prospect of marriage. But she adamantly insisted upon her own terms, refusing to be a child-bearing slave for any man she did not love and respect. Many a time her father's hall had echoed with their rousing arguments, brought about by her refusal to be a tool in some convenient alliance he was attempting to arrange. Despite her rebellious displays of temper, she knew it was her resemblance to her mother that had influenced her father to always reluctantly relent. Though marriage would separate her from her family, it would not have been a final separation, such as she now faced. That desolation made her more sensitive to Tokar's plight, and she felt a bond developing between them.

The old man appeared to be contemplating his reply. Then he spoke. "The time for secrecy has past. If I am to be of service to you, it is important that you know all." He met her inquisitive eyes evenly. "In gratitude for your father's intervention with the High Priestess, I ofttimes offered him my council."

Sheela shook her head. "I knew not."

"None did. I would will my mind body to appear before him in his chambers."

"Mind body?"

Tokar nodded. "It is something possessed by all, but few ever develop the power to use it. The mind temporarily separates itself from the physical body, assumes its own shape, and travels wherever you will to be." He smiled. "Though there are dangers involved, I much prefer that plane of existence. There my shape is as tall and spear-straight as the mightiest Thorgon."

Sheela again remembered the stories she had heard about this witch-man and decided his words were true. She asked, "Did my father heed your council?"

"On most matters," he replied. Then his pale, lined face became grave. "But he refused to heed my advice against a decisive battle with the Rhobians. Though I stressed it would end in disaster, he chose to accept the High Priestess' augury of victory. I implored him to speak with Lanzad, but he said he would have no truck with sorcerous apparitions."

"Who is Lanzad?"

"A demon who dwells in the third of Earth's twenty planes. He is a teacher, but imparts his wisdom begrudgingly. It was he who foresaw defeat. And it was by no accident that I happened upon the clearing where you met with the High Priestess."

Sheela was now utterly confused. Still, she continued to believe his tale. "He told you that she would attempt to kill me?"

Tokar nodded. "Furthermore, he said my efforts would be for naught if you decided to remain and continue the contest with the Rhobians."

She sat bolt upright, disregarding the blankets as they again slipped from her body. "I am to flee my homeland!"

"For a time. Only slavery and death await if you remain," he said solemnly.

Sheela's eyes blazed with indignation. "I'll not cowardly desert my people for the safe life of an exile!"

Tokar sighed wearily. "Spoken like King Heathgan's true daughter."

"Do not make light of me, Tokar!" she warned.

"I do not jest, my queen," he said simply. "But you will discover, as did your father, that noble words and deeds cannot alter what is destined."

"Like my father, I will stand and face all," she declared.

"When you fall, the remainder of our people will fall with you. And the Thorgons will truly be no more." Tokar's penetrating eyes bored into hers. "Is that what you wish?"

Sheela's anger began to wane; she sat in moody silence, unmindful of her partially naked body.

At length Tokar quietly continued. "Perhaps it would ease your reluctance if you spoke with Lanzad. Have you the willingness and courage to do so?"

Sheela looked to him sharply. "I fear not your demon!"

"Then I shall summon him this eve, and we will glean what knowledge we can from him." In response to Sheela's assertive nod, he said gravely, "But you must harken well to my words at all times, my queen. Lanzad is cunning and greatly dangerous. He will seek to entice you to cross our circle of protection, so that he may gain control of your soul and body. To achieve that end he will use any means—anger, trickery, or flattery. If you give in we are both lost, as he will then be able to invade the circle and slay us."

She scowled. "If he is that full of deceit, how can we accept his word?"

"Command him to speak truthfully and he is compelled to do so." He paused, studied her closely. Then he asked tactfully, "Had Your Highness rather I not summon Lanzad?"

Before Sheela could ponder her reply, her ego, which constantly reminded her that a queen must not show fear, spoke for her. "Call your demon, Tokar, and I will have words with him!"

Three long black candles in golden holders stood in the middle of a stone altar, their flickering light casting sinister shadows about the walls. Two sticks of incense sent twin spirals of thin gray smoke drifting up toward the lofty black ceiling. Before the altar Tokar recited an incantation in an ancient tongue, whose strange syllables were spoken when man first trod the Earth.

Standing several paces back, Sheela divided her attention between Tokar, whose gentle chanting was gradually building in intensity as he aroused his own inner forces, and a bench across the room where a flagon of wine and a gold cup had been placed. A low burning torch set in a wall niche illuminated that area with wavering specterlike shadows. The witch-man's voice rose, filling the small room and reverberating off the walls and down the dark passage to the main room. Sheela suddenly gasped, her amber eyes widening in apprehension, as a faint luminous mist appeared before the bench. Her eyes locked on the brightening, expanding mist, she edged nearer Tokar.

The old man's voice trailed off as he turned toward the churning mist, which grew thicker and began to assume a column-like shape. He regarded it for a moment, then spoke. "Lanzad, I command thee to show thyself to me outside this circle in a fair and human shape!"

Slowly the image of a face began to form at the top of the swirling column. It was a face of unearthly beauty. The mist abruptly vanished and in its place stood a very tall, perfectly proportioned, godlike man clad in a brief loincloth of a strange metallic type of fabric. His majestic beauty exuded confidence and arrogance; he was the epitome of the Thorgons' ideal of their gods.

Tokar smiled and said in polite amusement, "You have outdone yourself this time, friend Lanzad."

The godlike being eyed him with a sulky aloofness, then shifted his gaze to Sheela and very slowly took in every aspect of her tall, magnificent body. A smile of approval spread across his face. "I well understand your concern for King Heathgan's she-cub, friend Tokar." His eyes remained on Sheela as his sonorous voice purred, "She is most pleasing to the eyes. Do you wish my aid in slaking your lust with her?"

"Lanzad, you forget that she is my queen!" Tokar remonstrated, truly shocked by his suggestion.

"She is still a wench," Lanzad said, his eyes devouring Sheela. "And all wenches love to roll and kick."

Sheela's indignation overcame her nervousness, and she said coolly, "Your pet demon is most tiresome, Tokar. If foul talk of lust is all we may expect from him, then banish the creature back to his own realm where he may offend others of his own ilk."

The demon smiled. "Well spoken, most beauteous and haughty of queens. By royal rights my insolent behavior entitles you to come and discipline me." He bowed and said in a servile tone, "I place my humble self at your disposal."

Sheela looked at him narrowly. "Save your ruses, demon. I have been forewarned of what will befall, were I to leave this circle of protection."

Lanzad glanced to Tokar who smiled and nodded in confirmation. He arched an eyebrow in disapproval and gave a deep sigh. "You have displeased me greatly, old fool."

"But I have tried to make amends," Tokar said pleasantly and motioned toward the bench. "Knowing your fondness for wine while you are in our humble plane, I filched a flagon of fine Rhobian wine from a captain who no longer had need of earthly possessions." The demon hesitated, still scowling his discontent. Tokar continued. "I trust it meets with your approval."

Lanzad slowly turned and looked at the flagon. It raised into the air, dipped, and began to pour some of its contents into the gold cup.

As Sheela stared in fascination, Tokar moved to her side and whispered, "He seeks to impress you. Beware. He is taken with you and will not give up so easily." They watched the cup lift into the air and float to Lanzad's hand while the flagon gently settled back down on the bench. He drank, then shrugged indifferently.

"I am mildly content," he said, after another sip. "Now what do you want of me?"

"My queen wishes to regain her homeland from the invaders," Tokar said.

Lanzad sipped his wine and solemnly leveled his eyes on Sheela. "There is but one way. You must leave this night and follow the Volu River south to its end at the great desert canyon that separates the Northern and Southern lands. There in the Southern lands you are to learn the crafty ways of civilization, in order to become a wise queen, and make future allies to call upon when the time is right for you to retake this land."

"What assurance have I that your way is best?" Sheela asked aloofly.

"You are as proud and arrogant as your father," Lanzad replied harshly. "And like him, you would rule no better and come to the same end."

"My father was a good king!" Sheela retorted, taking a step forward. Tokar caught her arm and nodded down at the white chalk line several paces before her. Obeying his warning, Sheela planted her boot heels and glared across the line at the demon as she continued. "He stayed within his borders, made no false alliances, and all, save the Rhobians, feared to seek him in battle!"

Lanzad shrugged and said between sips of wine, "Your father let his land stagnate in his declining years. He was content with isolation, knowing and caring naught of the outside world. With the exception of what little trade he allowed to cross Thorgon boundaries, there was no change in his people's material belongings or way of life. It is a rule of nature that when a country becomes idle, its people are conquered by a more vigorous, creative people."

"The decadent Rhobians!" Sheela spat.

"They are still vigorous and wise in the ways of civilization. And despite your blusterings, my vain, lovely one, you are quite incapable of ruling wisely or well at this present time."

"Hold your insulting tongue, most foul of demons," she exploded, "lest I order Tokar to return you to your dung heap!"

To her further irritation, Lanzad only smiled and willed the flagon to float through the air and refill his cup. Then he said quietly, "Words of temper will not change the truth."

Sheela whirled on Tokar. "I will not deign to suffer this abusive creature's presence any longer. Away with him!"

"But, my queen . . ." Tokar protested.

"I will remain and lead my people to victory. Then all will see how well I rule!" She turned and icily glared at Lanzad.

The demon casually looked up from his wine cup and purred harmoniously, "It is only out of my deep regard for my dear friend Tokar—and his excellent wine, which I intend to finish before departing this petty, insufferable plane—that I make this final gesture to dissuade you from your folly, Queen Sheela. Cast aside your prejudices and look you well—for what you see is no deception!" He extended a hand toward her and a beam of radiant ruby light shot from it.

Sheela gasped and stepped back, catching Tokar's arm. The old man stood watching calmly as the glowing light sped across the room. Then, on reaching the white chalked line, it abruptly burst into a blinding ball.

A phantasmagoria of chaotic shapes swirled inside the gigantic ball. Slowly they became recognizable as Thorgons and Rhobians hewing and slaying one another in a mad blood-lust. Once again the courageous Thorgons went down in gory defeat, overcome by the staggering weight of numbers and superior armament.

Amid cheering throngs, a huge procession moved through the gaily decorated streets of Rhobia, a mighty, sprawling city with vast statue-lined streets and buildings as tall as towers. Sheela gaped in disbelief at the sight of herself, her wrists and ankles manacled in gold captive's chains, led behind the chariot of the victorious Rhobian commander.

The scene became a magnificent banquet room, where hundreds of officers and men of influence feasted at long marble tables. Slave girls, naked save for high-heeled sandals and gold chains about their wrists and ankles, moved about with gold trays containing vessels of food and drink and endured the men's brazen fondlings without protest. The girls were from all parts of the world, and Sheela gazed in wonder at their unfamiliar features. Some were white-skinned with oval faces and firm breasts; others, small and delicate, with yellow-hued skin, glossy black hair and curiously slanted eyes. Then there were girls as brown as the earth, and yet others as black as night, whose hair was short and tightly curled. She recognized some tall girls with pale or red hair as being from the Northern lands—and was then outraged and humiliated to see herself among them.

At a dais sat a short man wearing a slender gold diadem and a rich purple robe. His skin was soft and shiny pink, his hair dyed blond, and his face painted like a woman's. Sheela surmised that he was Flavio, the mad emperor. On his right sat his empress, a beautiful woman with icy, cruel features, dark cold eyes, and flaming red hair worn in a tall coiffure. Her nigh transparent robe was a mockery of convention and left little of her splendid figure to the imagination. On the emperor's left sat a young man with delicate feminine features and a very unmanly air about him. As the emperor appeared to be devoting more time to the handsome youth, Sheela decided that the stories about his preference for male lovers were true. She also noted that the empress seemed to be casting interested glances at the various slave girls.

Abruptly the feast became a mass orgy. Men and women rolled about amid the food on the marble tables; others did their love-making in the wide center area before the tables in a most depraved manner. Many of the slave girls willingly complied, but some vainly resisted. Accompanied by the youth, the mad emperor wandered among the rutting groups plucking a lyre and reciting poetry. The empress remained at the dais, casually eating and drinking while her eyes coolly swept the room, lingering on one group, then another.

Sheela saw herself struggling madly as a group of cruel-faced men took turns ravaging her lustfully. Though her cheeks burned with shame, a macabre fascination compelled her to continue watching the torments the men were subjecting upon her unwilling body.

The scene switched to an opulent private chamber, where Sheela saw herself hanging naked from an overhead beam by her wrists, her toes inches above the floor. Leather thongs cut cruelly into her wrists and ankles, which were connected to a ring bolt set in the marble floor.

Clad in only a brief transparent skirt and high-heeled sandals, the empress stood before a gold inlaid couch and lovingly flexed a long black whip as her eyes coldly caressed the tall beauty that helplessly awaited her pleasure. She flicked the whip expertly and was disappointed that her victim showed no fear. Then she slowly drew back her arm and sent the whistling lash streaking forward. Sheela jerked in her bonds but did not cry out as the whip coiled about her loins. It reluctantly slid away, leaving an angry red circle on her smooth golden skin, and slithered back across the marble floor.

Her face a mask of perverted passion, the empress slowly and sensually began circling the tortured girl. As the whip continued to sing its cruel song, Sheela's resolve broke. Screaming with every stroke, she twisted and shrank from the agonizing touch of the lash while the red-haired woman cooed and continued to vent her lust.

Spellbound, Sheela watched the scene's frightening climax. She saw herself dangling semiconsciously, her tear-stained face drooped between her extended arms, her slender body shuddering spasmodically. The empress, her sweat-drenched body glowing in the lamplight, stood clutching the bloody whip to her heaving breasts. Her breath came in quick, erratic gasps as her large glazed eyes roamed over the blood and sweat-streaked figure hanging before her, following the rivulets of blood oozing down the long graceful legs and tapered ankles to form a widening red pattern on the white marble floor below. Small shivers of excitement shook her lithe frame, and she backed to the couch and collapsed upon it.

She began to writhe in a frenzy of ecstasy, rubbing the long whip over her feverish body, and her mass of streaming red hair wildly lashed her wet face as her head tossed from side to side. Eerie pants and moans issued from her gaping scarlet mouth, growing louder and more urgent with her frantic movements. Then her body arched high in a sudden convulsive thrust and her chilling, animalistic scream of depravity filled the room. Her body poised, tense, statuelike, then abruptly crumpled back upon the couch, limp and spent, wrapped in the whip's supple embrace.

As Sheela stared in revulsion, her blood frozen in her veins, the room vanished and was replaced by a private indoor arena. Bright torches illuminated the large room as though it were daylight. Seated alone in the stands, the emperor's male lover giggled and squealed, his hands fluttering, bird-like, as he eagerly watched Flavio, dressed in a leopard skin, stalk about in a grotesque imitation of the animal before a dozen naked men and women who were bound, spread-eagle, to wooden crosses, set at intervals around the arena.

Roaring and brandishing the animal's front paws, the mad emperor launched himself at a helpless man. The sharp, slashing, renting claws dug deeply into the man's chest. The man-beast relished the agony he beheld as he slowly ripped downward with both paws and disemboweled the writhing, screaming victim. His eyes glowing with perverse glee, Flavio seized a long, loose strip of flesh between his teeth and tore it free from the man's body with a violent shake of his head. Growling and dangling the bloody trophy in his mouth, he turned from the dying man and looked up at the stands.

The youth gave a shrill shriek of mock horror and quickly hid his face in his hands. Then he slowly parted his long delicate fingers and peeked out at Flavio, who growled and shook his head, sending flecks of blood sailing about him. The youth lowered his hands and a wide smile of approval spread over his handsome face.

Pleased, the emperor's bloodsplotched features broke into a grin as he met the youth's eyes for a long moment. Then he shook his head and sent the strip of bloody meat flying, to land with the other gore at the dying man's feet. Turning, he roared and moved with graceless stealth toward his next victim—a tall beautiful girl with white-gold hair.

Sheela tensed, her amber eyes widening with shock and terror, her fingers digging into Tokar's forearm, as she recognized herself as the girl on the cross. The old man showed no pain and made no effort to disengage his arm from her strong grasp. Sheela watched in breathless horror as the fiend slowly approached the defenseless girl.

Flavio's smile was terrible to behold as he stood before Sheela and menacingly raised the deadly, bloody talons. She shrank at the touch of the warm blood dripping down onto her body and bravely tried to meet his eyes without fear. This amused the emperor who proceeded to toy with her, clawing the air and jumping about as his low growls slowly grew in intensity. The claws grazed her side and blood slowly oozed from the long scarlet rows. The sight brought a maniacal howl and Flavio's bloodlust exploded into a bestial fury. His eyes glazing and spittle drooling down the sides of his mouth, he struck out berserkly with both paws, ripping, tearing, slashing the beautiful vulnerable body to bloody ribbons.

Caught up in the unbelievable horror, Sheela screamed hysterically as she saw herself screaming and writhing beneath the cruel claws, and felt the agonizing pain searing through her body.

Then with a sudden swiftness the ball imploded in a violent ruby glow and the images dissolved.

Clinging to Tokar's arm, Sheela swayed on weak legs as she watched the bright shrinking ball evaporate before her eyes. Slowly she regained control of her emotions and stilled her shivering body.

Across the room, Lanzad looked up from his wine and smiled. "Now you have beheld your fate. It is not a very queenly one, is it my beauty?"

Her mouth dry with fear, Sheela turned questioningly to Tokar, who nodded and said, "The vision you saw was the same as I looked upon before. I beg you to take heed, my queen."

"Tokar means well by you," Lanzad said. "Though why—if not for your most splendid body—I fail to grasp."

Sheela found her voice and asked, "What awaits if I do leave this land?"

The demon shrugged. "Trials and hardships. But in time you will overcome them and someday victoriously return to your homeland."

"When will that be?"

He sipped his wine, then replied evasively, "That depends entirely upon how soon you have gained the necessary wisdom."

Sheela scowled, but the horrible vision was too fresh in her mind for. her to argue. "You say I am to follow the Volu River to its end—but I know naught of boats, and the land is hostile to strangers."

"A way will be provided," Lanzad said simply.

"How?" she demanded.

The demon drained his cup and sent it floating back to the bench, where it gently settled beside the empty flagon. Then he sighed deeply. "How wearisome you are. There will be a way, trust in that and be satisfied." A crafty smile stole over his face. "Come to me and I will whisper it in your delicate ear."

"No, demon," Sheela said firmly.

He eyed her with a wounded expression. "Since you trust me not, I shall depart."

Before Sheela could reply the demon vanished into thin air.

The Nomad Queen

"Trickery," warned Tokar as he looked about the dark room. "He lurks here, invisible, hoping we will leave the circle."

"Sheela!" a familiar voice echoed from the passageway.

Sheela spun around as a towering, robust white-haired man with a fierce mustache entered the room. "Father . . ." she gasped, staring in disbelief.

The man's battle hardened features softened, and he strode forward with outstretched arms. "My dearest Sheela! How I have searched for you!"

Tears welling in her eyes, Sheela moved to meet him.

"No!" Tokar shouted, lunging after her.

But Sheela ignored the old man and continued toward her father who stood waiting outside the circle of protection.

"Beloved daughter, come and embrace me!" the familiar voice urged anxiously.

As Sheela reached the white chalk line Tokar's desperate shout filled the room.

"That is not your father!"

Chapter Three

Sheela froze, her toes touching the chalk line, and stared up questioningly at the tall man before her; there was naught to denote an imposter. She felt Tokar's strong hand grip her arm as he hurried to her side.

"What means this, Tokar!" bellowed the familiar voice. The white eyebrows knitted in an oft familiar scowl, the gray eyes shone with menace, and the iron jaw clenched, grinding strong white teeth. "Why do you seek to keep my daughter from me?"

Sheela turned to Tokar and nodded in agreement. "You are mistaken. He is my father!"

"No, my queen," Tokar replied sternly,

"you are deluded. Lanzad stands before you in your father's image."

Stunned into speechlessness, Sheela turned back and again scrutinized the man.

The tall man scowled and gave a deep sigh of irritation. "Has age addled what brains you have, old man?" He extended a hand to Sheela. "Come, daughter, let us leave this old fool to his mummeries."

Tokar quickly drew Sheela back from the line. "I do not invite you, Lanzad, to enter this circle. But if you are King Heathgan, then you should be able to take your daughter from me."

"Sheela, we have no time for his childish games. Your brothers anxiously await us outside."

"They live?" Sheela asked, surprised.

The tall man grinned. "They are as fit as you."

Sheela stared into the trusting, magnetic gray eyes and felt herself compelled to believe this man that Tokar said was not her father. She started forward, reaching out her hand to his, but Tokar sharply jerked her back.

"Let him come to you," he cautioned. "The circle of protection does not bar any mortal's passage."

"Daughter, it grieves me that you would spurn your own father thusly," spoke the tall man, his face a mask of deep hurt and sadness.

Again, Sheela was compelled to go to him. "Release me, I must comfort my father!"

"Enough of this charade, Lanzad!" Tokar shouted, clinging to Sheela's arm. He raised his staff high in his free hand and said with every fiber of his being, "I command you by all the forces and the ancient Book of Gramobia to reveal yourself in your true form!"

The tall man reeled as though struck a mighty blow. Sweat poured from his brow, his strained face contorted in anguish, a soul-rending scream burst from his throat.

"Father!" Sheela screamed, breaking free from Tokar and starting toward the staggering man.

Abruptly the layers of human flesh fell away, and in King Heathgan's place stood a large hideous creature with bulging, red froglike eyes; saliva dribbled from its puckered lips, and a yellow slime oozed from its scaly brown and green body. It watched with sad, disappointed eyes as Sheela recoiled screaming in pure terror and turned away, burying her face against Tokar's chest.

"In my own realm I am considered quite

handsome," the demon muttered. Then he trembled with rage and extended a long scaly arm toward Tokar. "Curse you, old man!" he slobbered, his six-fingered, long-taloned hand curling into a menacing fist. "May you wither and—"

"Silence, demon!" Tokar roared, holding Sheela protectively and raising his staff high. "I grant you license to depart this realm in peace. You will forthwith return to your own plane; there to dwell until I have need to summon you again!"

"No!" shrieked the demon. "I would have the woman!" He threw himself at the invisible barrier, pounding, scratching, kicking, bellowing inhumanly.

"Lanzad, slave of my will," Tokar shouted over the creature's frustrated screams and hisses, "I command you to depart this realm—now!" He slammed the butt of his staff into the ground.

Suddenly a strange billowing cloud of dark smoke rose from the ground and engulfed the furious demon. With a final howl of rage and frustration, the horrid form faded into the smoke that drifted upward toward the high ceiling and began to dissipate.

Sheela and Tokar stood silently watching the last whisps of smoke vanish into the lofty blackness. Then he turned to her and said, "It is now safe to leave the circle. Lanzad is no longer present."

She blushed self-consciously. "It seems that I am constantly in your debt, dear Tokar."

The old man smiled. "I am merely more experienced in dealing with demons, my queen."

"You have my royal word that, henceforth, I will obey your every command without question, when trafficking with Lanzad."

"It would be best," Tokar agreed dryly.

They left the circle and returned to the main room, where Tokar produced a flagon of wine. "I feel we have need of a stimulant," he said as he filled two goblets. "Though the Rhobians be our bitter enemies, their wine is still most excellent."

Sheela accepted the goblet without protest and drank deeply. The wine was excellent, but her hatred for Rhobia kept her from commenting upon it. She moved to the firepit and stood staring down at the low crackling flames.

Tokar settled himself on a bench and made appreciative noises over his wine. Then he cocked his shaggy head and looked across the fire at Sheela, who stood lost in troubled thought, and said sympathetically, "I know the choice is hard, my queen."

"What choice have I?" she said bitterly. "Though I love my country and my people, I have no desire to end my days as your demon's vision has shown." She shuddered and took a deep sip of wine to help force the terrifying memory from her mind. Then she resumed watching the flames and smiled without mirth. "I leave my country, a queen who never sat her throne."

"You are young," Tokar said reassuringly. "There will be many years ahead for that. And when you one day look back upon these times, you may do so with a surprising fondness." He smiled at her dubious frown and raised his goblet. "Let us now drink to your safe journey—and to your triumphant return."

Distant lightning flashes lit the black horizon, accompanied by low rumbles of thunder. Sheela drew the wool cape tighter against the cold wind that swept the hillside path and held out her necklace to Tokar.

"Show this to my people, as proof that I still live. And tell all you are my sole representative. Any who dispute you shall answer to me upon my return."

Tokar nodded and took the necklace. "I will faithfully act on your behalf, my queen."

Sheela gazed fondly at the pale, wrinkled face that she had once dreaded. "You, dearest Tokar, are my most loyal and selfless subject—and the noblest of all Thorgons." She embraced him and kissed his cheek.

The wan light, cast by a sliver of moon that momentarily escaped the dark scudding clouds, revealed tears glistening in the old man's eyes. He drew his head farther back into his cowl, in an unsuccessful attempt to hide them, and cleared his throat several times.

"Your words are too kind, my queen," he said at last.

"They are true," Sheela said quietly. "And I humbly request that, henceforth, when we are alone you address me as Sheela."

"My queen!" Tokar gasped, taken aback by the breach of royal etiquette.

"You have more than earned that right. And I will be deeply sorrowed should you refuse my most sincere desire."

The old man beamed with pride. "Never would I purposely seek to distress my queen. I gratefully accede to your wish . . . Sheela."

Sheela smiled. "Thank you, my valued friend and protector." She touched her unscarred hairline as she drew the cowl about her head. "And most wonderous healer."

"That praise must be shared with Lanzad. It was he who instructed me in the healing arts."

"I prefer to give you my thanks," Sheela said dryly. Then a closer thunderclap interrupted their conversation, as if urgently reminding her of her journey.

"Nature seeks to aid you this night," Tokar said, glancing up at the dark sky.

She nodded. "The approaching rain should keep the Rhobians and other wild animals to their shelters. And if not . . . ." She patted the hilt of the sheathed short Rhobian sword that Tokar had given her.

"Your passage will be unmolested," the old man assured.

Sheela bent and picked up the sack of food and wine at her feet and slung it over her shoulder. "I must be off," she said with a reluctant sigh. "Farewell, Tokar. Oft will I remember you when I am in the Southern lands."

"Rest assured that wherever you be, my mind body will come and report any matters of grave importance," Tokar said.

Sheela nodded, summoned a smile, then turned quickly and strode down the path before her courage could falter.

Oblivious to the chill wind, Tokar remained watching the tall, straight figure of his queen until darkness swallowed it. He regretted not speaking of the many hardships that lay ahead; but it had been difficult enough to set her on this path and he could not risk deterring her. Queenship had its price, and there was naught else for her if she would be queen. The jagged streaks of lightning and crashes of thunder heralding the approaching storm seemed to ominously foreshadow his thoughts as the old man turned and, hunching his bent frame against the howling wind, slowly started back up the narrow winding path to his lonely cave.

Dawn found Sheela crouched behind a clump of bushes peering through the swirling fog and drizzling rain at a fierce horned dragon's head towering above her at the end of its long curved neck. Slowly the fog parted to reveal the strange black ship aground on the edge of a sand bar. The bottom of its great black sail had been partially burned and hung limply from the crossarm. Though over a dozen black shields lined its side, there were no sounds or movements aboard the ship.

River raiders from the far North, a land of eternal ice and gloom. Oft had she seen their long ships plying the mighty river on their grim incursions, bringing death and destruction to all they encountered. Had they learned of King Heathgan's death and come to pick the bones of his land before the Rhobians finalized their claim? If so, she must return and warn her sleeping people.

The fog continued to lift, and a large man was seen seated upright on a bench in the ship's stern. He was clad in splendid gold cloth apparel, complete with gold buttons, and a gold cloth cap edged with sable, upon which sat a gold square-cut crown. The pillows and spread he lounged on were of the same gold cloth, and his weapons, a long straight sword and double-headed battle axe, lay on either side of him. He appeared to be sleeping, his body rocking with the ship's lurchings as the swift current sought to free it from the sand bar, but the rigidity of his limbs betrayed death.

Sheela drew an easier breath. It was not a raiding party, but a king's death ship. She had heard tales of how these people sent their dead to the next world in fiery ships laden with their possessions and all that would be needed in that new life. Either the fire had not been properly kindled or the rain had put it out as the ship drifted down river, until caught on this sand bar. Lanzad had said a way would be provided for her to safely reach the Southern lands, and this must be it. There would probably be enough food and drink in the lockers to see her for the entire journey. And if there was a kingly treasure on board, she would easily make friends and allies in the South. Perhaps, she could return immediately with an army of mercenaries and rout the Rhobians from her soil.

Smiling, Sheela picked up her sack and hurried through the rain and fog toward the ship. Already the swollen river was beginning to submerge the sand bar and would soon set the ship free. The strong current lashed at her booted ankles, threatening to sweep her feet out from under her, as she made her way across the sand bar to the pitching, swaying ship. She abruptly stopped short and stood, heedless of the rain and driving current, staring up uneasily at the fog-shrouded black ship looming before her. She did not consider herself overly superstitious, yet she felt an icy foreboding course the length of her body. The prospect of a long voyage with a decaying corpse was an unpleasant one; it was tantamount to dwelling in a burial chamber before violating the spoils. Had the priests of the river people invoked some sorcerous power to protect their dead king? She had heard of such things; and her encounter with Lanzad had lessened her skepticism of forces beyond this world.

As though impatient with her indecision, the ship lurched farther onto the sand bar and lowered its side to her. Instantly she shrank back, clutching the sack to her breast as a frightened child would a doll of wood or rags, and almost lost her footing. The distracting struggle to maintain her balance against the swift current banished her trepidations. This monstrous thing of wood with its dead cargo could not harm her; it was the Rhobians, and the many tribes which bordered the river, she should fear. There was safety aboard the ship; not even the river raiders would interfere with its passage. Angrily chiding herself for her delay, she splashed forward through the rising water.

The ship's movements slackened as Sheela approached. Aided by the shields along its side, she managed to climb up over the gunwale. She hesitated, dangling one long shapely leg inside the ship, and cast a cautious glance about the deck. The benches were empty; the only sounds were the creaking of the rigging, the drumming rain, and the river slapping against the ship. She dropped her sack down onto a bench and followed after it.

There she crouched, hand on sword hilt,

eyes and ears straining to discern someone or something lurking in the fog, ready to challenge her intrusion.

Naught was seen or heard.

But why did the nape of her neck continue to prickle?

Slowly she stepped down onto the deck and, throwing back her rain-soaked cape, drew the short Rhobian sword. The sharp rasp of steel rang from stem to stern, announcing to any unseen assailant that she was armed and ready. Reassured by the feel of the blade, she started along the rows of benches toward the raised stern where sat the dead king. The sound of her high-heeled boots on the slippery deck seemed magnified sixfold in her ears, but it disturbed not the sleep of the dead.

Through the wisps of fog she could see boxes and bales stacked about the king's bench, along with the bones of dead horses. Curiously, a black dog, instead of its bones, lay at the king's feet. The smooth-coated brute was the size of a cave bear cub, with massive jaws and hanging lips. It appeared once powerful and deadly, and Sheela was greatly relieved that it was dead. Then, as she drew nearer, an unearthly phosphorescent glow appeared in the beast's large eyes. Slowly the great head lifted from between its paws and bared long cruel fangs in a silent snarl. Its throat hung ragged and open—the thing was dead, yet possessed with life!

Despite the rain, Sheela broke out in a cold sweat; her spine felt as if grave worms were crawling and slithering up and down it.

The creature stiffly rose to its feet and, hackles bristling, advanced to the few steps leading down to the deck.

Scarcely breathing, her eyes wide with uncomprehending horror, Sheela backed away. But the beast launched itself at her in a long leap, its hideous fangs snapping for her throat.

At that instant the wet deck pitched beneath Sheela's feet and she went down flat on her back. The dog sailed past above her, hit the slippery deck and slid its full length before coming to a halt. Nails furiously clawing the deck, it turned and, eyes glowing like beacons, charged back through the fog.

Sheela scrambled to her feet and bolted for the steps. The wet deck impeded the dog's rush, and she gained the stern ahead of it. She tore off her cape and flung it into the beast's face as it started up at her, then put all of her might behind a thrust to its ribs. The sword sank to the hilt and she twisted savagely.

There was no effect upon the creature.

With a toss of its huge head, it shook away the cape and whirled on Sheela before she could withdraw the wedged blade. Desperately she retreated, scattering boxes, bales, and bones in its path. Yet on it came, eyes glowing, fangs glinting, sword hilt grotesquely protruding from its side. A box against the gunwale blocked her further retreat, and the dog slowly moved in for the kill.

Seizing upon a frantic plan, Sheela jumped atop the box and stood looming above the gunwale. "Come and take me, sorcerous fiend!" she taunted.

As if in answer, its red maw opened wide in a soundless growl and the animal bounded up at her. Sheela threw herself aside and the beast's momentum carried it over the gunwale and out into empty space. Then there was a resounding splash.

Sheela regained her feet and leaned over the gunwale. She saw the phosphorescent orbs glowing like twin balls of evil beneath the roiling water as the strong current swept the beast down river. Weak with relief, she sagged against the gunwale and stared after the rapidly diminishing glow. Then the ship gave a sudden lurch and, with a scraping of its bottom, rode over the sand bar and was carried on its way by the rising water. The unexpected movement flung Sheela sideways into the box, an instant before a hissing axe stroke cleft the gunwale where she had stood. The head bit deeply into the wood, sending forth a great shower of splinters. That mighty blow would surely have parted her in twain to her navel. She stood rigid, staring in shocked surprise at the figure before her.

It was the dead king!

Two black eye sockets, picked clean of their contents by birds of prey, looked back at her. The pallid face bore other deep pock marks of their horrid work and white bone showed through in many places; the lipless mouth was drawn back in a cadaverous grin above the full gray beard. His nerveless hand effortlessly extracted the double-headed axe from the wood and raised it high for a killing stroke. The sweet-sour odor of death and embalming powders assailed her nostrils as he stiffly approached.

Self-preservation snapped the invisible bonds of fear that held Sheela rooted and she leaped aside as the deadly axeblade descended. It missed her bare shoulder by less than an inch and crashed into the box, which spewed forth glittering riches. She spotted the long sword still upon the bench and made a frantic dash for it. Fast on her heels came the corpse, the axe singing its song of bloody death as it whirled above his head. She snatched the sword and spun, lifting it in a blind parry at the sound of his tread behind her.

Sword and axe instantly collided with a ringing metallic clang, and the violent vibrations almost sent the hilt flying from Sheela's stinging hand. Desperately she gripped the hilt in both hands and hastily backed away as the dead thing attacked with an unrelenting frenzy.

Sparks flashed like lightning in the fog as axe and sword met repeatedly in a ringing tattoo that echoed out across the water. Unable to do more than turn aside the whirling axe, Sheela nimbly avoided tripping on the scattered animal bones, gold coins, precious jewels, and other riches which littered the rolling deck as the keen blade smashed boxes and bales in its savage pursuit. Sweat ran down her brow and a deep ache set into her muscles; still the cadaver came at her untiringly, with the axe whistling and singing its bloodthirsty song of destruction. She knew she must end the battle quickly, before her remaining strength fled—but how did one kill what was already dead?

Again the king leaped in, lowering the arc

of the axe in a mighty backhand swing at Sheela's stomach. She felt it hew the air, almost touch her skin as she leaped back, then brought her raised sword down in a two-handed stroke at his other brawny arm. The blade sliced through bone and dried flesh, neatly taking the arm off at the shoulder.

The stroke would have downed an ordinary man and left him writhing and gasping out his life in his own blood. But there was no blood and this was no ordinary man. He merely paused, axe raised, and turned vacant black eye sockets down at his severed arm lying among the glittering riches on the wet deck. Then his head swiveled to cast a malevolent eyeless gaze upon the tall, pale-blond girl who stood staring in awed disbelief, and, swinging the axe in great back and forehanded swipes, he renewed his attack.

Parrying furiously, Sheela fell back step by step with each battering blow. She skillfully eluded a stroke that passed an inch over her head, and thrust two-handedly at the cadaver's massive chest. The sword sank in half its length, lodged against the spine—and during that instant before it was withdrawn, an axe stroke nearly parted Sheela's head from her lovely shoulders.

Unnerved by a one-armed corpse with a

gaping hole in the middle of its chest battling her unfalteringly, Sheela resigned her soul to whatever fate, if any, awaited her beyond this life and, screaming in rage and frustration, abandoned all in a berserk fury. Her sword flashed in wild slashes and swipes, meeting the axe strokes with an equal force. Lost in a red haze, she let her instincts guide her in eluding the dead thing's return strokes and continued to press her attack. She feinted a parry but dodged under the blow instead and, as the axe whisked past her ear, struck at the thing's leg, lopping it off below the knee.

Axe raised for another swipe, the corpse stood motionless for a moment, then abruptly toppled sideways on its unsupported side. Desperately thrusting the axe into the deck, it braced its fall and landed on its knees. The lipless mouth opened wide in a soundless scream and the eyeless pits glared wrathfully as the corpse violently reared up, raising the axe.

Sheela quickly swung the long blade in a sweeping semicircle, felt it cleave through the bull neck, shattering muscle and bone, and the corpse's head flew through the air.

It landed atop the gunwale with a meaty thud and bounced high into the air. The cap and gold crown fell over the side, revealing a bald, wrinkled pate, as the head hung suspended in midair, mouth opened, black pits seemingly expressing surprise. Then it swiftly plunged downward into the waiting water.

The splash brought Sheela's attention back to the headless torso kneeling before her, axe frozen in mid-swing. Taking no chance that it still might possess supernatural life, she chopped off the hand. Still gripping the axe, it spun in the air and fell to the deck. With both hands she raised the sword high and brought it down in a mighty slash.

The sword bit into the headless neck, tore downward through the middle of the torso, hewing spine and chest bones, until its point stabbed deeply into the deck and sent vibrations coursing up the length of Sheela's arms. The corpse shuddered, then divided in twain, and reluctantly fell away to either side of the blade. Sheela wrenched the point free and continued hacking furiously. Only when the corpse was scattered in over a dozen pieces did she stop.

Taking the large gold cloth from the bench, Sheela gathered the pieces, a few at a time, and dropped them overboard. She watched the cloth sink beneath the water with the last remnants of the corpse and gave a relieved sigh; at last she was undisputed mistress of the ship. She surveyed the glittering riches littering the deck and smiled. Truly it was a king's fortune. Her destiny was now assured, and she would soon return a conqueror. Content with that knowledge, she turned and stood staring back at the great forest of her homeland until it was lost from sight.

Sheela woke to the distant, ever-growing roar of rushing water. For a long moment she was content to luxuriate in her warm bed of furs and ponder curiously. Then, reluctantly forcing herself to throw back the heavy robe, she sat up. All about her the air was filled with spray. Shivering, she immediately reached for the robe, but the sight ahead made her forget the damp chillness.

Before the dragon-beaked prow stretched a long seething current of racing water. And beyond, barely discernible through the rising mist which sparkled a multitude of colors in the dawn light, lay the source of the thunderous sound—a great waterfall.

Sheela sprung to her feet, only to be hurled back down upon the furs as the swift-moving ship heaved and rocked mightily. Staggering, crawling, avoiding the sliding, tumbling boxes and bales, she frantically made her way across the reeling deck to the tiller and, bracing herself erect against the gunwale, grasped it in both hands. A glance at the nearest bank showed her the incredible speed at which she was traveling. The grassy plain and rolling hills beyond flashed past in a dizzying blur as the madly rushing river collected itself for its inevitable plunge over the fall. Sheela flung herself on the tiller in a desperate attempt to bring the ship toward the bank.

The long ship lurched and swayed, writhing in the churning current like a wounded serpent. Gray water came boiling over the bows and onto the deck as the raging current swung the stern around, heaving it up and dipping the dragon nose, and sent boxes and bales careening in wild confusion. For a terrifying moment Sheela feared the ship would be swamped. Then the prow reared high and the ship went flying broadside down the river.

A huge box shot straight across the deck at her. She fled from its path an instant before the box slammed against the tiller, splintering it into fragments, then caromed off the gunwale and skidded on its way, leaking a trail of riches behind it. Sheela hurled a sulphurous curse after the destructive box, but the roaring rapids deafened her ears to her words.

Had a trick of the current brought about this accident, or had an unseen sorcerous hand sent the box hurtling into the tiller? She had no time to waste in speculation; the racing current increased with every yard, bearing the doomed ship onward toward the edge of the fall. There was naught to do but abandon it to its fate and take to the water.

Sheela looked toward the bank, saw the rocks and lodged drift dotting its shore, and the slack water at the edge of the furious current. To reach that calm safety she must thwart the current's will and traverse twenty yards of frothing water. The chance was slim; but surely drowning would be an easier death than what awaited below in that thundering chasm. She cast a lingering glance about at the vast wealth that had been hers for a sennight but was now lost. The swim would be most arduous and she dared not chance even the slightest burden. Cursing her misfortune, Sheela left the ship in a long stretching dive that carried her a quarter of the distance she must cover.

The icy rushing water shocked her senses, threatening to numb her limbs. Shuddering with cold, she started to break for the surface. But the frenzied current hit her with the force of a battering ram, tumbling her head over heels in a series of somersaults, and sought to drag her back from the shore and farther into its chilling embrace. She lost all bearings as she frantically wrestled the enveloping frigid tentacles of the swift, deep current. Her straining lungs tightened, jerked spasmodically. She needed air most desperately. She must breathe *soon* or die.

Pressing her lips tightly shut, she determinedly fought back the gagging spasms in her throat, denied the impulse to gasp for breath. There was naught but icy water which would fill her mouth and lungs, strangling her. Her body convulsed, her vision blurred, her mind grew dim . . .

Then high above she saw a shaft of sunlight penetrating down through the foamy water and, with an urgent kick, she shot upward like an arrow. The light grew brighter; frantically she drove for it; still her thrashing hands met only water. Her body demanded air, her tortured lungs were nigh to bursting. Great invisible weights seemed to burden her weary limbs. She must pause and give them rest.

No! screamed her primitive survival instinct.

Reluctantly she obeyed, thrusting her spiraling body upward through the rushing turbulence. With every stroke, every kick, the light above brightened, yet remained elusive. It was now impossible to further refuse the desire to breathe. Her reason no longer heeded the consequences. *She must breathe.*

Slowly her lips parted.

Then she crashed through the surface and up into the radiant sunlight, her body rising half its length out of the water; a golden water goddess appearing to pay homage to the sun. Her open mouth deeply drank in the moist, life-giving air, quenching the fire in her lungs. Its taste was far sweeter than the finest of wines.

Without a struggle Sheela rode the swirling current until her senses gradually returned. The deafening din of the fall reminded her of the danger, and she urgently took her bearings. She was well over a dozen yards from the edge of the current's trough and the still water beyond. The bank seemed to race wildly along with the river and vanish over the fall with the same suddenness. Beyond that stretched naught but the shimmering, billowing mist.

Far ahead of her, trapped in the midst of the wildest part of the current, the dragon ship steadily swept toward its doom. So rapid was its movement that the long ship almost appeared to be standing still. Then she saw something that chilled her far more than the icy water.

Silhouetted against the overhanging mist, a wavering, semitransparent figure stood solemnly looking back at her from the stern. It was the dead king's ghost, come to reclaim his treasure. Or had he been there all the while, patiently awaiting his chance. The fierce, malicious glow of triumph in his eyes made Sheela again speculate about the accident to the rudder.

Her thoughts were suddenly interrupted as a small hard wave broke against her face. Choking on a mouthful of spray, Sheela forgot all else but her own peril. Urgently she began to breast the current, stroking and kicking with all of the strength she could summon. Though she seemed to move with incredible slowness, each stroke brought her slightly nearer to the bank.

On Sheela stroked, battling the furious current for every foot, every yard. Her limbs ached with fatigue, her whole body felt leaden. The roar grew louder in her ears as the current relentlessly carried her closer to the edge of the fall; already wisps of mist were beginning to gather about her. Then ahead she saw a branch protruding above the water from a pile of drift bordering the still water and the bank beyond.

If she could catch the branch as she was swept past, there was life. Should she fail a horrid oblivion awaited at the bottom of the waterfall.

Cresting the current, Sheela gathered what strength remained in her exhausted body. Then, almost before eye and mind could register and react, she was to the branch. Blindly she threw her arms upward, felt the bark's slippery wetness beneath her grasping hands, and frantically sought purchase. Her straining arms momentarily halted her body's forward movement against the surging water as she edged nearer the drift.

Then her hands slipped!

A trick of the current slammed Sheela's struggling form sideways and sent her skimming over the low barricade into the calm water, where she floundered, hacking and spewing. Then she found her footing and reeled through the waist-deep water to the bank.

At the touch of solid ground beneath her feet, her body surrendered to its fatigue. Sheela pitched forward onto the damp earth and lay greedily gulping the forest-scented air while her body jerked with uncontrollable muscle spasms, like a freshly-landed fish. The tremors finally passed and she weakly drew herself up onto an elbow. Brushing a plastered stream of wet white-gold hair back from her face, she looked toward the thundering waterfall.

As though it had been waiting for her eyes to see, the dragon ship was perched on the lip of the fall. The ghostly figure still lurked in the stern and appeared to be laughing uproariously. For an instant the ship floated on the multicolored mist and then abruptly vanished below the fall, taking with it Sheela's dreams of a swift return and an easy conquest of her homeland.

With tear-filled eyes, Sheela stared forlornly at the empty mist. This great disappointment broke down all barriers, and the human emotions she had denied herself since that day of disastrous defeat by the Rhobians burst forth. She flung herself down and, pillowing her head on her arms, sobbed with wild abandon.

When, at last, her eyes were dry Sheela felt a great calm. The tears had unburdened her from all past sorrows, and she was now able to begin this new life unencumbered. Despite whatever tragedies lay ahead, it would be a very long while before she again allowed herself tears.

As she removed her boots and shook the river from them, Sheela dispassionately assessed her situation. She was in a strange land—alone, afoot, unarmed, and, worst of all, without a coin in her possession. Very bleak prospects, indeed. Yet she had bested all obstacles to come this far, and there was naught to do but continue onward. She knew not how, but, by all the gods and forces that might exist, she meant to accomplish her goal. The intensity of her determination sent new strength surging through her weary limbs.

Sheela struggled into her boots and rose. Then, with a confident stride, she began following the river bank and disappeared into the swirling mist.

Chapter Four

She had reached the Volu River's end, and now stood before the great canyon that separated the Northern and Southern Lands. The first step of her journey was completed.

Awestruck, Sheela stared at the majestic waterfall roaring down into the deep arid canyon stretching endlessly before her. Somewhere far below, in the rising mist that obscured the canyon floor, lay the ship and its treasure. Perhaps one day she would find a way to reclaim it, but now there were more urgent matters. Her hands, pressed tightly against her ears, were unsuccessful in shutting out the deafening roar of the water, and if she did not soon leave here she would surely lose both her senses and her hearing. She turned away and, moving southward, began skirting the side of the canyon. Even when she had gone some distance, the sound of the waterfall remained inside her ears. Otherwise, she might have sensed the danger sooner.

Sheela was deaf to the flat snap of a bow and the whistling arrow's flight until it was almost upon her. It thudded before her, halting her in mid-stride. She instantly whirled, her keen eyes scanning the tall grass and dense woods beyond.

Chilling war cries broke the stillness, and five riders brandishing lances charged from the nearby trees. As they drew nearer, she was surprised to see that they were women, clad in boots and brief clothing of fur and leather. With no hope of escaping the shrieking, thundering horsewomen, she fiercely returned their war cries and ran to meet the lead rider.

Abandoning herself to her primitive instincts, the tall, pale-haired Thorgon girl's slender body became a graceful flurry of motion. Nimbly avoiding the woman's thrust, she caught the lance and yanked her down upon her back with a most audible *thump*. Before the stunned woman could rise, Sheela slammed the lance butt into her jaw and swiftly ended her participation in the battle.

Swinging the lance like a staff, she then unhorsed the second rider, and blocked a spear point as the third galloped past. She spun, saw the fourth woman bearing down upon her, then side-stepped and, dropping into a crouch, shoved her lance between the horse's front legs.

Screaming in unison, both horse and rider crashed heavily to the ground. The shaken horse struggled to its feet, but its rider lay motionless.

Quickly replacing her broken lance with the unconscious woman's weapon, Sheela pivoted, ducked under the fifth rider's thrust and, with both hands, swung her lance up, striking the woman mightily across her back as she rode past. A sharp cracking of ribs accompanied the sound of the blow and the screaming woman fell from her horse. Ignoring the shrieking wench writhing in the dirt, Sheela dove aside as the third woman returned and attempted to ride her down.

Rolling to her knees, Sheela drew back her lance for a throw as the woman tightly wheeled her horse around. Then she abruptly became aware of other hoofbeats. Out of the corner of her eye she caught sight of a sixth horsewoman and started to twirl. She was too late. A lance butt slammed against the side of her head.

And darkness embraced her . . .

Pain and a sense of motion were Sheela's waking sensations. As the vertigo and nausea diminished she became aware that she was tied across a horse. A rope joining her bound wrists and ankles together under its belly tugged sharply with each step. A chorus of female groans distressed her aching head, but she took grim satisfaction in the knowledge that she had caused their sufferings.

A woman's voice spoke in sharp irritation. "Cease this childish whimpering. It does naught to stop the pain and is false comfort."

"Your reprimand comes easily, Zambra," a shrill voice whined. " 'Twas not your ribs she broke!" Several other voices joined in agreement.

The one called Zambra spoke again. "Yonder lies our camp. I will not be disgraced by leading a pack of sniveling wenches. You will act like warriors and bear your wounds in silence, until you have reached the privacy of your tents!"

Reluctantly the women stifled their moans, and the group rode on in silence.

Feigning sleep, Sheela slightly turned her head and cautiously parted her lashes, hoping to glimpse the camp, only to find herself peering into a tangled maze of her own cascading white-gold hair. Suddenly a hand roughly seized her hair. Sheela involuntarily gave a cry of pain and surprise as her drooped head was jerked up and twisted, her neck bent almost to the breaking point. Her wide amber eyes stared up at the cruelly smiling face of the rider whose saddle she was tied behind.

The woman was attractive, with high cheekbones and almond eyes that slightly tilted upward at the corners, yet there was a cold hardness to her features. Her long, disheveled red hair, hanging well below her shoulders, caused Sheela to remember the Rhobian empress and shiver at the memory. "So our pale-haired lioness seeks to deceive us by shamming sleep," spoke the taunting voice which Sheela recognized as belonging to Zambra. The group halted and Zambra addressed them. "Did not her cry salve your wounds?"

"My dagger across her throat is the only salve," spoke the girl with the broken ribs as she glared at Sheela.

Zambra laughed mirthlessly. "That would be an easy death. You lack the proper imagination, Oda."

"Give her to me and then judge for yourself!"

"She is too valuable a slave to be wasted on your petty revenge." Zambra smiled, amused, as her captive's large amber eyes flashed defiantly. "Our lioness is proud. That is well." Her fingers twined tightly in Sheela's hair, but the defiant expression remained. Slowly she loosened her harsh grip. "Release her from my horse. She will walk behind me as my captive."

One of the women dismounted and quickly severed the rope connecting Sheela's wrists and ankles. Then, with an almost casual jerk of her arm, Zambra roughly flung the helpless Thorgon girl backward from the horse by her long hair.

Sheela sought to dig her boot heels in as her feet struck the ground, but her numbed ankles refused to support her. She continued her fall backward, and her head met the ground, hard. Stunned, she lay unresisting as the woman deftly looped a long rope between her bound wrists, and attached the other end to Zambra's stirrup.

Zambra turned to the group. "Go ahead of us and inform Princess Sumara of our coming, then see to your wounds." She stared after the eagerly departing group, then rammed her spear into the ground and dismounted.

Helpless, Sheela apprehensively watched her approach. In her soft, red leather, high-heeled boots, Zambra appeared a hand's breadth taller than her. The two strips of tawny fur about her full breasts and shapely hips revealed a lean, firm, well-muscled body; she would be a formidable opponent. She stopped beside her and stood, legs apart, hands on hips, somberly scrutinizing her. Sheela felt most uncomfortable under her lingering gaze. After a long moment, Zambra spoke.

"I am Zambra, commander of a mercenary band presently in the service of the Princess Sumara. You have heard of me?"

Her question was answered by a blank stare.

The flame-haired Amazon shrugged in dismissal and said, "I was muchly impressed by your fighting skills—such praise I do not bestow lightly."

The Thorgon girl's beautiful face was impassive.

The tall woman continued. "I am willing to intercede on your behalf and ask the princess to give you to me."

Sheela flared indignantly and struggled to sit up. "I am Sheela, Queen of the Thorgons. No one has the right to *give* me to anyone!"

Zambra quickly pinned the girl's shoulder to the ground with a boot heel and, with casual cruelty, ground it into her tender flesh. "Queen or not, you are now *my* prisoner—and naught but a slave."

Sheela glared up at her with cold hatred, her wrists and ankles straining futilely against their taut bonds.

Very slowly Zambra eased the pressure and said softly, "You will not move again until I command you to do so." She withdrew her heel and smiled at the angry red mark on her captive's golden skin. Then her lingering gaze swept over Sheela's magnificent form. "Your beauty equals, if not surpasses Princess Sumara's. Hard will be your lot, for she is most vain. You would be wise to accept my offer."

Sheela's obstinate pride refused to heed caution. "I take orders from no one, neither do I follow!"

Zambra only smiled coldly and shrugged as she drew a knife from her thin belt, then leaned over and, with a quick slash, severed the rope about Sheela's ankles. Replacing her knife, she turned on her heel, strode back to her horse, and mounted. She yanked her lance from the ground and called to Sheela, who was staggering to her feet. "You are now a follower!" She nudged her horse forward.

Her ankles still numb, one leg buckled beneath her on her first step and Sheela almost fell. The taut rope jerked her upright and tugged her onward, further brusing her slim wrists.

Zambra walked the horse for a short distance, then gradually increased its pace. "Let us see how well you follow!" she called, urging the horse into a canter.

Sheela felt the rope yank harshly on her outstretched arms, threatening to tear them from their sockets, and desperately forced her reluctant legs to obey. She ran, her heart pounding, her breath coming in pants. It was a valiant effort, but she could not stave off the inevitable. She fell and, her struggling body rolling over and over, was dragged along the ground. Then, abruptly, her torment was ended, and she lay still, amid a trodden and crushed patch of tall grass, dazedly squinting up at the early morning sun.

"On your feet, *Your Highness!*" commanded the flame-haired Amazon's taunting voice.

Though her whole body was a mass of pain, common sense overrode Sheela's defiance and she staggered to her feet. No sooner did she stand, swaying like a drunkard, than the horse moved forward, and there was a sharp tug on her throbbing wrists. Biting her lower lip, to deny her captor the satisfaction of her outcry, she winced and stumbled on her way. To her relief, Zambra was content to walk her horse at a leisurely pace, and the remainder of her march was somewhat more bearable.

They entered a narrow pass, guarded by four women warriors who shouted greetings down to Zambra, and soon emerged into a wide clearing where a large camp stood. As she was led along a winding row of tents and rude huts, Sheela recalled Lanzad's vision, in which she was led in gold chains through the cheering streets of Rhobia. Though this was not the same, her cheeks still burned with shame and humiliation. She curiously noticed small groups of men, their ankles chained, meekly performing menial chores, while groups of women warriors drank, gambled, and practiced with various weapons. Surprisingly, none of the groups appeared much interested in her arrival. She also noticed the lack of children and old ones in the camp. That was a blessing, for they were usually the cruelest to captives, hurling sticks and stones, and venting their own frustrations of inadequacy by devising other fiendish torments.

They left the area of tents and huts and approached a large brightly colored tent, guarded by a group of women warriors, set apart from the rest of the camp. Zambra halted near the entrance and threw a glance back at Sheela who stood swaying on her feet; only sheer will-power kept her from collasping in exhaustion. Several guards moved forward as the flame-haired Amazon beckoned.

"Secure the captive until Princess Sumara deigns to decide her fate!"

Too weak to resist, the tall Thorgon girl allowed them to lead her, most urgently, to a nearby post and firmly lash her in place, with ropes twined about her, from her neck to her ankles. Then she was left to ruminate upon her fate, while Zambra disappeared inside the huge tent.

How long she stood there, she did not know. It seemed truly an eternity. Despite herself, her mind persisted in thoughts of gloom, and her situation did naught to dispel them. She had traveled to the Southern Lands with high hopes, only to have them dashed, most cruelly. Lanzad had spoken of learning the crafty ways of civilization—if this was civilization, then she wanted none of it. These people were just as barbaric as those of the Northern Lands; and she could not envision her fate being any the more gentler than what she had beheld at the hands of the Rhobians. Then she heard a stirring and incoherent voices inside the entrance of the tent and shifted her eyes in that direction.

A tall, slender, ivory-skinned woman with long raven hair regally emerged from the tent, and was followed by Zambra and several scantily-clad male and female slaves, whose wrists and ankles were manacled in gold chains. Again the vision of herself similarly manacled and serving at the Rhobian victory banquet came to mind, and Sheela tensed indignantly at the thought. Had she come all this way, only to end her days as a slave?

Her every movement bespeaking her royal position, the raven-haired woman gracefully approached, with her entourage trailing behind at a respectful distance. The midmorning sun reflected off her gold cape, breastplates, girdle, bracelets, and gilded high-heeled sandals, with thin golden thongs wrapping her slim ankles, and caused Sheela to blink and avert her eyes from the glittering figure. She stopped before Sheela and regarded her aloofly. Summoning what dignity she could, Sheela met her stern, penetrating gaze directly.

Zambra had not lied; Princess Sumara was the most beautiful woman that Sheela had ever beheld. She not only equaled her in height, but in beauty, though Sheela's vanity would never allow her to admit such heresy aloud. Her firm, splendid body proved that she was no indolent royalty, pampered on silken cushions, but a warrior princess. At this close distance, she also saw that Sumara was no more than two summers older than herself. Her features were delicate, yet above her high cheekbones, her large deep blue eyes, rimmed by long sable lashes, reflected an inner strength. Her exquisitely molded red lips were pursed in a frown, and, long accustomed to the jealousies of other women, Sheela immediately sensed that the beautiful princess considered her a rival. And when Sumara spoke, her voice confirmed Sheela's suspicions. It was pleasant, but coolly condescending.

"I am told that you claim to be of royalty?"

Though Sheela sought to reply in the same cool tone, her parched throat conspired against her, cracking in mid-sentence and spoiling the desired effect. "I am Queen Sheela . . . of the Thorgons." To her further distress, all, save Sumara, tittered derisively at her announcement.

"I am not familiar with your people," Sumara stated indifferently.

Reminding herself that she was in these Southern Lands to win allies to her cause, Sheela bit back a sharp retort and said simply, "We dwell in the Northern Forest Lands."

Sumara nodded. "One of the barbarian tribes." This time her retinue laughed heartily. Sheela shifted her eyes from Sumara and glared at them. Then Sumara's voice again claimed her attention. "Why are you so far from your home?"

"I came in search of allies to aid in driving the hated Rhobians from my land."

Sumara's eyes widened; evidently she was familiar with the Rhobians. She considered a moment, then shook her head. "A fruitless task. None, save fools, will go against the might of Rhobia." What scant hopes Sheela had held were dissipated by her words. The princess beckoned Zambra forward and said, "By the look of your warriors, this slave resisted fiercely."

"She is an excellent fighter," the Amazon said. "She unhorsed four of my best warriors."

"I can use such a fighter." The raven-haired princess looked directly into the Thorgon's girl's eyes. "Serve me well in my upcoming battle against King Jator of Istwar, and I will grant your freedom when I am ruler."

"As a queen, I serve none but myself!" Sheela replied indignantly.

Sumara tensed as though struck, her lovely face scowling her displeasure. Clearly, she was unaccustomed to rejection of any sort. When she spoke, her haughty voice was scarcely above a whisper. "*I* am the only royalty here. You will serve me, either as a warrior, or a mere slave. But serve me you shall!"

"Never!" Sheela declared, meeting Sumara's icy blue eyes with equal resolve.

For a long moment, all sound and movement around them ceased as the two women stood glaring at each other. Then, not taking her eyes from Sheela's, Sumara addressed Zambra.

"Take her to the Land of the Thirsty Death. She shall have until sunset to reflect upon her decision."

"But that is a fate reserved for deserters," protested the tall Amazon.

Sumara whirled on her. "Obey me!."

"At once, Your Highness," Zambra said, bowing slightly.

Sumara turned on her heel and imperiously stalked toward her tent. Her retinue hastened after her.

Zambra looked to Sheela and said quietly, "You were warned."

Her anger still on the rise, Sheela disregarded her and watched Princess Sumara disappear into her tent. Though she knew not how or when, one day their positions would be reversed, and she vowed to repay the proud princess twofold, for the treatment she received at her hands.

Inside the deep, parched desert canyon, Sheela was stripped bare by three women, while Zambra looked on. Then she was thrust, face down, upon the warm, coarse white sand, before a narrow stream, and intricately bound, from her shoulders to her crossed ankles, with rawhide thongs. But the women were not yet done. A long length of rawhide was dunked in the stream. Then one end of the dripping thong was attached to her crossed ankles, and the other end around the trunk of a lone, gnarled, stunted tree, where her boots and clothing had been placed. She quickly discovered that the rawhide securely held her head back a scant inch from the narrow stream before her. Their task completed, the women turned and moved toward their horses.

Zambra strode to the Thorgon girl's side and stood surveying her helplessness. "Soon your body sweat will wet your bonds, which will contract as they dry, cutting into your flesh and adding to your other torments." She smiled tauntingly and shook her head. "I do not envy your experience till sundown."

Though deeply worried, Sheela did her best to appear stoic and ignore her words. It was no simple matter. The Amazon squatted beside her, grasped a large handful of her hair and roughly turned her head to look directly up at her.

"I well understand pride," she said solemnly, "but there comes a time when one must cast it aside." Her almond eyes stared into Sheela's. "If you will not serve the princess, then join my band and I will shield you from her wrath. You will ride at my right side." She paused and regarded her for a long moment before continuing. "Consider your answer most carefully this time, for never again will I extend this offer of friendship to you."

Sheela's anger and stubborn pride once more intervened over logic. "I am a queen, and no one's underling!"

"So be it!" Zambra exclaimed, her face fully expressing her wrath. She roughly shoved

Sheela's face into the sand and stood. "We will see how arrogant you are after the sun has done with you, *Your Highness*!" She gave the girl a mighty nudge with her booted foot, turning her over onto her back, and scowled down at her. "From this time on, we are bitter enemies—and long will you regret your decision!"

Shaking the sand from her face and spitting grit from her mouth, Sheela tried to match her angry stare; but the blinding sun above the Amazon's shoulder caused her to wince and squint her eyes. Zambra turned and strode to her horse, where the other women, already mounted, waited. Sheela grimly watched her swing up into the saddle.

"Farewell, till sunset!" Zambra jeered. Then she and the others wheeled their horses and galloped away, leaving the helpless pale-haired girl to her solitude.

As Sheela stared after the departing riders and listened to their horses' fading hoofbeats, her anger was slowly replaced by consternation. She had now made a powerful enemy of Zambra—that she did not regret. However, the long hours she must pass in the sun might give her second thoughts. *No!* It was not in her nature to be subservient, especially to one not of royal birth. And as far as Princess Sumara was concerned—may the ice giants devour her!

The sun was hot upon her face, and it was most uncomfortable lying on her tightly bound arms. She tried to roll over onto her stomach, but immediately found that movement was much more easy to contemplate than to accomplish. Pushing with her hands and turning her legs, she managed, with great difficulty, to twist onto her side, and from there, roll over onto her stomach. The effort had been tiring; she was both sweating and breathing heavily.

Aware that time was her enemy, Sheela began to writhe, testing her bonds. The leather thongs bit tightly into her tender flesh. Her long slender fingers fluttered, seeking to get a purchase on the tight knots confining her wrists, only to learn that they were tied close, in between her wrists, well out of reach. After a few more tries she gave up and lay still, hopelessly pondering her plight . . .

The noon sun cast its fiery rays down upon the desert, whose white sands hurled them back with an equal vengeance. High up in the cloudless azure sky, three vultures circled lazily, keeping a patient vigil over the motionless figure that lay beside the glimmering stream.

Suffering marred Sheela's exquisite features. Her large amber eyes stared longingly at the tantalizing water, scant inches from her parched lips. She knew she must drink—and *soon*—before the sun greedily sucked every drop of moisture from her tall, magnificent, golden body. Already the sweat-soaked rawhide thongs imprisoning her were drying and contracting, biting deeper into her flesh and adding to her torment. Once more she craned her slender neck toward the elusive water, straining to the utmost every fiber in her body. She grimaced as the effort immediately sent shocks of pain through her slim ankles and up her long lovely legs. Then the fast-drying, long length of rawhide connecting her ankles to the gnarled, stunted tree contracted, drawing her naked body back, another inch from the stream.

Trying to divert her mind from the unobtainable water, Sheela grimly cursed this strange land and its inhabitants—especially Princess Sumara—Tokar and Lanzad, for sending her on this fool's quest, and, most of all, herself and her faults, which she began to realize were many. Under other circumstances a brief indulgence in self-pity might have been comforting, but here, baking under the merciless sun and almost delirious with pain and thirst, it was a futile

114

endeavor. Sheela again set her dull mind to the task of scheming a way out of her predicament. She knew not how, but she was determined to escape before Zambra returned for her at sunset.

Squinting into the spider web maze of her disheveled white-gold hair, Sheela saw a tawny shape approaching through the rising heat vapors, on the other side of the stream. At first, she thought it a specter of her sun-addled brain, but as she watched, it took the form of a cave lion. She had often seen pelts and drawings and heard stories of the vicious cats, but this was the first living one she had laid eyes on—and her helplessness doubly intensified her terror. She forced her numbed body to make a final frenzied assault on her bonds, but the sweat-soaked knots had dried into small, tight, impregnable leather balls. Scarcely breathing, she lay trying to control her quivering form as the enormous cat stopped on the opposite bank and stared at her.

For eons, neither moved.

Then, not taking its yellow eyes from her, the beast lowered its huge head and began lapping at the water. Though Sheela thought the sun had drained her, she felt a cold sweat break out from every pore as she met the large sinister eyes unblinkingly.

After drinking its fill, the lion regarded her for an endless moment, then started to turn away.

Suddenly the long strip of rawhide contracted again, sharply jerking the girl back from the water. The lion whirled, ears back, snarling, poised to spring.

Immediately the scene of Flavio, the mad Rhobian emperor, in his leopard skin raking her helpless body with its paws in a bestial frenzy, flashed into Sheela's mind.

Then a ragged scream erupted from the pale-haired girl's dry throat as the beast, slaver dripping from its monstrous jaws, launched itself at her.

Chapter
Five

An arrow suddenly screamed through the air and sank deeply into the air-borne creature's loin. With a tremendous roar of pain and rage, the lion crashed into the stream, its huge claws raking the bank, narrowly missing Sheela as she rolled aside. While the great cat floundered, howling and snapping at the arrow embedded in its side, the Thorgon girl turned her head and saw a horseman, his cape billowing in the wind, fitting another shaft into his bow as he raced toward her along the bank. Relieved, she willed her bound body to obey and began squirming back toward the tree. The maddened beast turned toward her, but a second arrow buried into its side, distracting it completely.

As he galloped past between Sheela and the lion, the rider swung his bow with both hands. There was a sharp *crack* as the stout wood collided with the brute's skull and broke in two. The stunned lion reeled and splashed about crazily. The rider wheeled, rode behind Sheela, then leaped from the saddle and drew his long sword. With a quick stroke, he severed the long thong tetering her to the tree and ran toward her. The lion's thunderous roar caused him to veer away, shrugging off his empty quiver and hurling it as the beast started out of the stream. The leather case struck the lion full on its muzzle; it directed its attention to the tall, dark-haired man.

Slowed by the arrows, the enraged beast bounded at the man, who held his ground until the last moment, then lunged forward and drove his sword into its massive chest. The long blade sank to its hilt, neatly impaling the brute, and the man threw himself aside. A shower of sand flew wildly in all directions as the lion hit the ground and thrashed in its death spasms, clawing at the air and snapping at the sword hilt. Its paws striking blindly, the massive beast rolled toward Sheela who lay watching in helpless terror.

Again the image of Flavio slashing her bound body with leopard claws flashed before her eyes, and she tensed, awaiting gory destruction.

Suddenly the tall man bolted through the blinding cloud of sand, snatched her up in his strong arms, and leaped toward the opposite bank an instant before the dying lion was upon her.

Landing short of the bank, the man slipped and fell backward with a huge splash. Cold water shocked Sheela's dulled senses. Then she was urgently shoved from atop the stranger, who sat up hacking and sputtering in the waist-deep water. They looked back as the lion's huge body gave a final spasmodic shudder, its sinuous tail thumping the ground.

And then, abruptly, it was still.

The stranger heaved a relieved sigh and grinned at Sheela who, now that the danger had past, was attempting to lower her face to the water and drink.

"We may yet see the sun set this day."

Sheela nodded absently, her mind intent upon the still unattainable water. The man caught water in his cupped hands and brought them to her lips. She drank without hesitation, savoring its coolness as the life-restoring liquid glided down her parched throat. It was gone all too quickly, and she looked to him imploringly. But, to her disappointment, he gravely shook his head.

"You must drink sparingly. Too much at once will bring sickness—and even death."

Before Sheela could protest his wisdom, the man stood and drew her wet, naked body up onto the bank. Throwing off his soaked cape, he plopped down beside her and shook the water from his face and hair. She managed a smile.

"I am grateful for your most timely arrival."

The man motioned up at the circling vultures. "They must share your gratitude. Were it not for them, I would not have come to investigate."

"I am more inclined to give my thanks to you."

"And I am more inclined to accept them." He grinned and brushed a plastered stream of white-gold hair back from her face. "Who are you—and what was your offense, to deserve such punishment as this?"

"I am called Sheela." Caution made her refrain from telling him of her queenship. Also, his admiring gaze made her suddenly

aware of her nakedness and complete helplessness. She glanced away, attempting to
conceal her uneasiness. "And I defied Princess Sumara."

The man nodded and drew a knife from
his boot. "Ah, that explains all." He gently
turned Sheela sideways, with her back to
him, and carefully began cutting the tightly
knotted thongs from her body. "The bandit group I was with—until last night—has
crossed swords many times with that ill-
tempered wench and her Amazons."

Sheela tensed, glancing back over her
shoulder at him. "You are a bandit?"

Sensing her uneasiness, he paused in his
work, and his dark eyes met hers. "Only by
necessity. I am Alon the mercenary. I fell
upon hard times, and had hoped to win the
bandits from their leader, Velor, and form
my own group of mercenaries."

"But you failed."

Alon shrugged. "They were an uncivil lot
anyway." He turned his attention back to her
bonds.

Sheela sat, carefully unmoving, while the
sharp blade deftly severed the many thongs
from her wrists, arms and torso, leaving her
skin untouched. As each thong fell away,
feeling returned to that area, in the form of
hundreds of fiery pinpricks. Partly to divert

her mind, she asked, "What are your plans now?" She was thankful that he kept his eyes on his work as he answered her.

"At the moment, I have but one plan— to avoid capture by Velor and his bandits." He cut the last thong from her torso and shifted his position to begin on her legs and ankles.

Sheela modestly would rather have performed that task herself, but her hands were far too numb to accomplish anything, save self-mutilation. She soothed her modesty by reminding herself that her handsome rescuer had already had ample time to admire her nakedness, and began the painful task of rubbing the circulation back into her limp arms.

His task finished, Alon replaced the knife and stood. Already the sun had partially dried his loose silk shirt and snug, soft leather breeches. "Now, if you will excuse me, I must see to my sword and horse." He smiled and added, "They are a mercenary's best friends." He turned and splashed back across the stream, leaving her to begin her ministrations on her aching legs.

When her limbs had sufficiently recovered, Sheela put on Alon's cape and crossed the stream, to fetch her boots and clothing. She dressed before the tree, then joined him at the stream, where he was filling a water bag while his horse drank.

"I dare stay no longer," he announced, as he stood and began tying the bulging water bag on his saddle. Sheela nodded and held the cape out to him. Alon shook his head. "You've had enough sun this day." He started to mount, then abruptly paused, eying her, his handsome face ill-concealing his distress.

Sheela stared back at him questioningly, saw him rigidly stretch his lean, muscular frame to its limit, and understood. In her slender-heeled boots, she now stood two fingers taller than him. Though she thought naught of it, Alon's manly ego was apparently most upset by that. As she had no wish to discard her boots or go about stooped over, there was but one thing to do—she resorted to her womanly wiles.

Summoning her most charming of smiles and fixing her large, innocent amber eyes upon his, Sheela again thanked Alon for her rescue, and commented with awe upon the immense size of the cave lion. Secretly amused, she watched him thoughtfully stroke his thin mustache as he studied the lion for a long moment. Then he grinned and grandly praised his accomplishment. Sheela nodded earnestly at his words, and remembered the many times she had successfully used such a ploy upon her father and brothers. But, to her dismay, he then turned back to his horse and once more prepared to mount. She wanted to call out to him, but her pride kept her silent; it was not right that a queen should beg.

Alon looked down at her and awkwardly asked, "Where are you bound?" She shrugged and looked about at the mean, desolate terrain. He frowned. "Have you no family or friends?"

Sheela shook her head and looked like a lost little girl. "I am from the North Lands."

Alon pondered, then gave a deep sigh of resignation. "I did not save you, only to abandon you to the tender mercies of Sumara, or Velor and his men." He leaned down and extended an arm to her. "You may ride with me to the first city we come upon—should no misfortune befall us."

Smiling radiantly, Sheela took his arm, swung gracefully up behind him, and they rode away.

Their patience finally rewarded, the three vultures swooped down and began to feast upon the lion's carcass.

Midafternoon found the two resting on a narrow trail near the crest of a shrubless mountain. Looking back at the hostile landscape below, Sheela pointed toward a large group of individual dust clouds and announced, "There are riders in the far distance."

"That will be Velor and his band." Alon quickly stood. "I had hoped his men would rebel at entering the Land of the Thirsty Death." He glanced up at a group of rocks. "If we can but block this trail, we will delay them greatly." The Thorgon girl stood and followed him up into the rocks.

It took time, effort, and much sweat before the large rocks finally crashed down onto the trail. Pleased with their task, the two resumed their journey.

The terrain on the other side of the mountain was equally harsh and barren, and the only water was an isolated salt lake. Hanging like a fiery copper ball in the cloudless sky, the sun continued to conspire against them every step of the way. Driven by the deadly knowledge of what was behind them, Alon and Sheela forced themselves and their tired horse ever onward, refusing to surrender to the blazing sun or the dry desert air that sapped their energies.

It was almost dusk when they saw the distant walls of a city, and galloped forward with renewed spirits. But as they neared the walls, the sunlight's last glimmer revealed that the city had long been abandoned.

"A dead city!" Alon said dejectedly, reining in the wheezing horse before the crumbling walls. He glanced back at Sheela, who nodded grimly. Then he shrugged. "Still it offers us shelter for the night."

Sheela eyed the shadowy towering walls uneasily. "I'd as soon stay out here."

Alon grinned. "Spoken like a true North Land barbarian." He nudged the tired horse forward, and Sheela, annoyed by his remark, sullenly kept her forebodings to herself.

As they rode through the gaping arch that was once the city gate, the horse's hoofs, echoing on the broad, broken pavement, seemed startlingly magnified by the stillness. Rubble and the occasional crumbled fronts of buildings littered the wide street, and it was obvious that, before the ravages of time, the city had fallen to a besieging army. Though an ominous aura shrouded the dead city, Alon and Sheela's sharp eyes detected no movement in the surrounding ruins. They continued on, to a more preserved section of palaces and temples, and camped in a wide courtyard.

Sitting on the marble steps before the great facade of a palace, they ate sparingly of Alon's meager rations. Sheela stared across the shadow-haunted courtyard at the silent, ghostly buildings, pale in the moonlight, and shivered, drawing her cape tightly about her. But it was a chill that even the hottest of fires would not warm. She sensed something evil lurking here, biding its time to strike. Yet she said nothing, fearing her worldly companion would dismiss her trepidations as merely those of a superstitious barbarian mind. Seeking distraction from her gloomy thoughts, she remarked, "I have never been in a city before. My people have always shunned them."

"That is their loss. Many more delights are to be found there than in a barbarian camp."

Though his words irked her, Sheela knew they were most likely true. Still, why did everyone in this Southern land regard those from the Northern lands as ignorant barbarians? Putting aside her regional pride, she asked, "Can knowledge be found there?"

"Certainly . . . all sorts," Alon replied. "What do you seek?"

"I seek the wisdom of a queen."

He regarded her with amusement. "You have lofty ambitions."

Sheela flared indignantly. "I *am* a queen."

The handsome mercenary broke into uncontrolled laughter. "I fear too much sun has addled your brain." He placed a hand to her forehead. She angrily swatted it away and fixed him with a withering stare.

"I am *Queen* Sheela of the Thorgons."

Her pronouncement was greeted by a blank stare. Then he asked dubiously, "Why did you not tell me this before?"

"I wished to know you better before taking you into my confidence."

Alon nodded. "Ah, I see . . ." But his face clearly expressed that he did not.

Attempting to conceal her wounded dignity, Sheela continued her explanation. "My land has been seized by Rhobian invaders, and I am in need of an army to free my people."

"And you want my help."

"I was foolish enough to think so," Sheela said haughtily, "but I now see I was mistaken." She regally gathered her cape about her and looked away. There was a moment of silence, then Alon was heard fidgeting and clearing his throat self-consciously; evidently he was now having second thoughts about his boorish behavior. Another moment passed Then his deep sigh of resignation was heard, and she felt his gentle touch upon her shoulder.

"Sheela, I—" his voice began, only to halt as she rudely shrugged off his hand and remained turned away, still deep in her sulk. He made another attempt. "I'm sorry.

It is only that I've never been this familiar
with a queen before." His tone was sincere,
so Sheela abandoned her sulk and slowly
turned to him. But before she could speak,
they were startled by the horse's shrill, dying
scream.

Instantly, Alon leaped up and, sword in
hand, charged across the shadowy courtyard;
Sheela was fast at his heels. They halted at
the edge of the courtyard and gaped in surprise at the fallen horse.

Its head had been neatly severed from its
body.

Their eyes sweeping the darkness beyond
the courtyard, they stood tensely listening.

All was silent.

There was no stirring.

Then they heard the tread of many light
footsteps, the creaking of leather, and the
rasping of blades, drawn from metal scab-
bards. Suddenly the dark streets were filled
with hundreds of small twin flames, growing
brighter as they approached, and the eerie
moonlight revealed the figures of armed
men.

"Back to the palace!" ordered Alon, taking her wrist, and Sheela complied without
hesitation.

Across the courtyard they went, and up the
marble steps to a set of large bronze doors,

standing slightly ajar. Time had done its work on the hinges, and the doors refused to move. Unable to squeeze through the space between them, Alon and Sheela desperately threw themselves at one. Groaning in protest, it swung inward several inches, but still not enough for them to pass. They turned and froze, staring in disbelief at the chilling sight before them.

The courtyard was half-filled with warriors, clad in ancient lacquered leather armor, baggy pants and soft leather boots. Their heads were naked skulls, with flames dancing inside black eyeless pits. Swords drawn, they stood silently observing the two living beings, while other warriors scrambled atop the crumbling walls surrounding the courtyard. With a creaking of dry joints rubbing together, one warrior raised his curved sword and stepped from the terrifying assemblage. His grinning jaws clicked open and shut in a horrid, mute war cry, then he charged across the courtyard.

Alon and Sheela remained transfixed as the nightmarish semblance of a man approached, clothes flapping about its shriveled, mummified body, and bones rustling with each movement like dry twigs. Regaining his wits, Alon grimly ordered Sheela to continue trying the door and bounded down to meet the dead thing as it started up the broad marble steps.

The courtyard resounded with clashing steel as Alon and the warrior's blades engaged in a rapid series of strokes and parries, and the staccato, gonglike rumble of the bronze door as Sheela frantically assaulted it with kicks and shoves. The warrior's furious onslaught forced Alon to reluctantly retreat back up the steps. Alon's blade slashed through the leather armor, revealing strips of withered flesh clinging to brown bones, but the warrior, twin flames glowing brighter inside his vacant sockets, only pressed his attack with greater intensity. Alon was almost to the top step, when Sheela called that the door was open. He parried madly, then saw an opening and drove his sword straight through the warrior's heart. But the body writhed savagely upon the blade and would not die. The clawlike hand raised its sword for a cut at Alon, before he could withdraw his sword.

Sheela rushed to the top step and, remembering her battle with the dead king upon his death ship, lashed out with one foot, in a sweeping kick. Her narrow boot heel snapped the brittle neck bone and the skull leaped high into the air. The twin flames abruptly died inside the skull as it twirled in midair, then bounced down the marble steps. The headless body went limp on Alon's sword. He wrenched the blade free and the clattering body rolled down the steps after its skull.

As another warrior raced across the courtyard, Alon and Sheela whirled and ran to the bronze doors. Seeing their quarries escaping, the other warriors charged after the lead warrior. Alon hastily squeezed between the doors after Sheela, and they struggled to close one as the lead warrior charged up the steps. Slowly, reluctantly, the door inched forward and slammed shut with a deafening *clang,* crushing the warrior as he sought to enter.

With the doors reverberating loudly under the other warriors' relentless attack, the two ran along a wide dark corridor, through several large, rubble-strewn chambers, and came to a broken archway leading out onto a broad avenue. No warriors were in sight, and they dashed toward the buildings lining the other side of the silent avenue.

Staying to the deep shadows, they ran along the pillared portico of a building, up the steps, plunged through its doorless portal, and found themselves in a vast room lined with slender pillars. Moonlight streamed through the lofty ceiling's broken dome, revealing the scattered bones of several skeletons around the remnants of a campfire. They swiftly made for a flight of stairs on the far side of the room, but suddenly froze as an ultra-high-pitched sound emanated from the high rafters. There was a leathery swish of wings, then a giant bat, with a seven-foot wingspread, hovered in the light from the broken ceiling.

"A carrion bat!" Alon shouted, seizing Sheela's arm and pulling her toward the stairs. The room was filled with the beat of wings as the monstrous creature swooped after them. Alon jerked Sheela to the dusty marble floor, narrowly avoiding the sharp claws on the bat's grasping, elongated fingers as it swept past above them. They were on their feet and running, while the bat circled the large room, which resounded with its shrill cries and flapping wings. As they reached the stairs the thing was upon them, but Alon's slashing sword forced it to veer away.

They were midway up the stairs when the bat again attacked, heading straight for Sheela, who ran ahead of Alon. Dropping into a crouch, she kicked sideways and felt the heel of her boot crack several bones in the creature's body as it was about to envelop her within its great black wings. Her forceful kick sent the shrieking bat sailing backward. It dipped, almost crashing to the floor, but recovered, madly thrashing the air with its wings. Reaching the landing, Sheela ducked inside the narrow archway and, gasping lungsful of air, looked around for her companion.

The bat intercepted Alon as he reached the landing, its long blunt muzzle open, fanged teeth ready to rend and tear at his throat. Alon put his weight behind a mighty two-handed sword stroke. The sharp blade cleaved through bone and membrane, completely severing one great wing from the huge furry body. With a piercing squeal, the creature spiraled downward, crashed onto the hard marble floor and flopped about crazily in its death throes. Alon started to turn, but heard the thrashing of another pair of wings and looked up to see a second bat gliding through the broken dome.

"Do not just stand there, woman—run!" he shouted to Sheela, who lingered in the archway. Frowning at his breach of royal etiquette, she hastily obeyed and he rushed through the archway, only paces ahead of the soaring creature.

As they ran along the dark passage, they glanced behind them and saw the huge bat fold its wings, drop down on all fours and scurry through the narrow archway. Hampered by the blackness, they ran on, feeling their way along the wall, while the passage echoed with the horrific shrieks of the pursuing bat who rapidly closed the distance separating them. Sheela's fingers encountered a doorway and she ducked inside, yanking Alon after her. They slammed the copper door and shot the bolt into place an instant before the bat hurled its massive body against it, claws furiously raking its surface.

The sturdy door withstood the violent assaults, and the two relieved humans looked about at their surroundings. A shaft of light from a narrow window reflected off the marble floor, dimly illuminating the small, bare room. Moving to the window, they looked down upon the broad avenue and saw the grim figures of the long-dead warriors skulking about in search of them.

Alon turned from the window. "We appear safe for the night." He wearily sank down, his back against the wall.

"As long as the door holds," Sheela said wryly, dropping down beside him. She grimaced and tried to close her ears to the harsh rasp of the bat's sharp claws upon the copper door. It was most maddening and set her well-frayed nerves on edge.

As the abrasive clamor continued endlessly, Sheela was tempted to seize Alon's sword and march out and do battle with the monstrosity—that was preferable to sitting meekly and waiting to be slowly pushed to the brink of madness.

Suddenly, when her overwrought nerves could take no more, the frustrated bat finally abandoned its efforts and left.

Sheela and Alon exchanged relieved glances as they sat listening to the wondrous silence, piecing their shattered nerves together once more. Then they closed their eyes and slowly surrendered to their great fatigue.

The ensuing quiet brought undisturbed sleep . . .

Chapter Six

The next morning Sheela awakened surprised to find herself snuggled in Alon's arms, her head resting on his chest. Trying not to rouse him, she self-consciously started to disengage herself, only to discover that he was awake.

"Good morrow," he announced cheerfully.

She awkwardly drew away from him and asked, "Why did you let me sleep?"

"I've never held a queen in my arms. It was most enjoyable."

Sheela blushed. "Your shoulder was a most comfortable pillow."

"I'm pleased it was to your liking." He stood and stretched, then extended his hand to her. "Shall we see what new amusements await us this day?"

Memories of last night's horrors vividly flooded Sheela's mind, but in the bright sunlight they now seemed less real. She took Alon's hand and stood.

Cautiously they left their sanctuary and retraced their steps. They found the bare skeleton of the first bat, then saw the second bat, too bloated to fly up to the rafters, clinging upside down to the edge of a lower stair step. As a precaution against another nightly confrontation, Alon quickly dispatched the sleeping creature with a swift stroke of his sword. A most unsporting, but most necessary act.

Returning to the palace courtyard, they found no sign of the long dead warrior they had fought. Their water bag and rations lay untouched.

"At least our friends left us our food and water," Alon said, sitting on the steps. "I am ravenous, and you?"

Sheela nodded and sat beside him. "Must you refer to them as our friends? I certainly feel no friendship toward the infernal creatures that inhabit this cursed place."

Alon handed her a piece of dried meat and took one for himself. "I have found that when in a perilous situation, it is always best to retain your sense of humor."

Sheela eyed him curiously. "It helps?"

Alon shrugged. "Sometimes."

They fell silent, eating and drinking lightly. When they had finished, Alon gave a weary sigh and looked about at the ruined city, which appeared no more hospitable in the sunlight. "Without a horse we will soon be overtaken in the desert by Velor. There is no choice but to await him here. If we can avoid capture until night, the skull-headed warriors may dispose of him and his men for us."

"What if he has given up the chase?"

"Velor never gives up on anything."

Sheela was thoughtful, reluctantly reconciling herself to their longer stay within the city. "Then if we must wait, let us see what knowledge we can glean of the skull warriors."

Alon nodded. "It will offer some amusement to help pass the time." They stood and started back to the broad avenue.

Inside the main temple they found several skeletons sprawled in awkward postures of death around a large stone altar, its smooth surface covered with a great dark smear, on which lay a female skeleton. Three towering half-human idols, their hideous, spectral white faces chipped and broken, stared down impassively. Though oily smoke stains had crawled up their legs, the three naked bodies still retained their corpse-blue paint. To Sheela they were a most unpleasant and unnerving sight and inspired no reverence.

"It appears the priests made a last desperate effort to beseech their gods' aid for the doomed city," Alon observed.

Sheela shivered. "What manner of people would revere such ugliness as their gods?"

Alon shrugged. "Perchance we shall find out in the king's palace."

Surely enough, Sheela's question was answered on the frescoed walls of the throne room in the king's palace, which depicted a pale, copper-skinned race of tall, graceful people with proud, austere faces. Armed with lances and round shields, soldiers in bell-shaped tunics and conical helmets fought long-haired warriors in heavy animal skins; hunting parties stalked birds and animals, many now long extinct; and dusky captives bowed in submission before a monarch and his resplendent court.

Sheela moved about, staring in wide-eyed fascination at the lavish court scenes, whose opulence reminded her of Lanzad's vision of the Rhobian court. She took grim comfort in the thought that if so grand and powerful a city as this once had been could fall to an invading army, then so could Rhobia. She smiled, imagining herself at the head of an army, standing before the city gates of Rhobia. Then a scraping of stone startled her from her thoughts and she whirled to see Alon standing in the doorway of a hidden passage behind the raised throne. Curious, she went to join him.

Peering inside, they saw sunlight, filtering through a collapsed section of the roof, reflecting off a bronze door at the end of the dust carpeted passage.

Alon grinned broadly. "Come, we may yet find some treasure in this place." Though she doubted it, Sheela cautiously followed him inside, and along the passageway.

The sagging door creaked eerily as Alon pushed it open and tensed, his hand going to his sword hilt. The light revealed the figure of a man, seated behind a marble table. But there was no danger; a long sword protruded from the middle of his chest. They entered the small room and moved to the table.

The man's withered hands clutched the sword, its hilt braced against the table's edge, and it was apparent that he had taken his own life.

"This one wasn't one of our nightly visitors," Alon announced, "his head is still intact."

Sheela stared down at a sheet of crumbling parchment before the mummified figure, who was less than average in stature. The rust-colored writing was in an archaic script. She shook her head and looked to Alon. "I am unfamiliar with this language."

He studied the parchment. "It appears to be an ancient form of Turanian."

"Can you read it?"

He shrugged, continued studying the parchment, then abruptly looked up in surprise at the man and burst into laughter. Sheela began to wonder if he had gone quite mad.

"What humor does it contain?"

Stifling his laughter, Alon made a sweeping gesture to the dead man. "This is Randar the wanderer!" Sheela looked blankly at the dead man. Alon frowned. "Surely you've heard his exploits told around the campfires? He's the hero of men and boys everywhere!" She shook her head and continued to look blank. Alon sighed. "Well, *almost* everywhere. With each telling, he grows taller and mightier, and his deeds become bolder." He smiled and shook his head. "What would his admirers say if they could see this apish caricature of a man?"

Sheela shrugged and delicately brought the conversation back to the parchment. "Is there any mention of the skull-headed warriors?" Alon leaned over the parchment and began to read aloud:

"I, Randor the wanderer, came to this cursed lost city of Baalshazzar in search of fabulous treasure . . ." He broke off and grinned at her.

"Go on," Sheela urged anxiously, her face lighting up with interest.

Alon resumed reading. "Instead, I found only the skull warriors, of which I had been warned." He and Sheela exchanged disappointed glances; then he gave a disgusted sigh and continued: "They were the personal guard of Bresar, son of Sikkim the conqueror, who had been killed during the siege of the city. In his grief, Sikkim denounced the warriors as cowards and had them beheaded. His shaman cursed their souls, and their only release from this city is to fight valiantly, in single-handed combat, all those who enter here. It matters not the outcome of the contest, as long as a warrior proves his courage he is freed from the curse."

"That explains why they left our food and water untouched," Sheela said. "They want us to live to fight them."

"I can think of more pleasurable pastimes."

"I heartily concur," Sheela said dryly.

Alon looked back to the parchment. "Misfortune has been with me since the first night. My horse was slain, and my leg was broken in a leap from a rooftop. The skull warriors come nightly, and I fight them until dawn." Alon heaved a sigh of disgust. "This is what we have to look forward to!"

"Isn't there any other way to be rid of them?" Sheela asked apprehensively.

Alon hurriedly scanned the parchment, then nodded and read aloud. "There is but one way to dispose of them: find their burial place inside the city and burn their corpses. My leg has prevented me from making an extensive search, and now my end is near. For three days and nights I have been without food and water, and my strength is gone. I have chosen to die by my own sword, rather than grant one of these fiends release by killing me.

"I have written this account in my own blood, in hopes it will serve whoever finds it. I ask but one favor in return. Should you escape my fate, never divulge my sorry end. Let the world believe that Randar the wanderer has ridden off in search of adventure in some far distant land, and will someday return with exciting tales of his brave deeds.

"I hear footfalls in the corridor. They are coming for me . . ."

"Poor man," Sheela said, eying the dead man sympathetically.

"It will be *poor* us—if we do not find the warriors' resting place, and Velor does not arrive this night."

"Regardless, let us keep his secret," Sheela urged. She saw his surprise and added, "It is a simple request. And we now know the warriors' secret."

Alon considered, then, with a show of indifference, tore up the parchment. "We would not want this to fall into Velor's hands," he said, scattering the pieces about the room. Aware that was but one reason, Sheela was careful not to smile. Men became flustered by their acts of sentiment.

They paused in the doorway for a final glance at the hero who had met the fate of a mere mortal, then closed the door, and began a long, futile search through the dead city.

Late afternoon found Alon and Sheela surveying the silent city from one of its high walls. "It will take centuries to find their gravesite," he said in disgust.

The Thorgon girl sighed and looked up at the dimming sky. "The sun will soon set."

They exchanged dire glances, aware of what awaited them at nightfall, and started to depart. Then they suddenly caught sight of a huge dust cloud moving out from behind a grouping of dunes. As it rapidly approached the wall, men and horses became visible within the cloud. Alon turned to Sheela and grinned confidently.

"Good old Velor." He took her arm. "Shall we prepare to welcome him?" They hastened to the stairs and descended.

From a rooftop that overlooked the palace courtyard, Alon and Sheela watched as the large cluster of horsemen rode vigilantly along the street. On entering the courtyard and spying Alon's dead steed, the party began nervous speculation among themselves. Dreading the hushed city, they were of a mind to consign the fugitive to his lot; but a brawny, red-bearded giant of middle years, clad in leather, gold chains and armlets, threw his swirling cape, grasped his sword hilt and threatened to slay all who tried to desert.

"That is Velor, despoiler of women and defiler of temples," Alon whispered. "He loves naught better than to take a woman upon a temple altar." The uproar below grew more noisome.

"They fear the city more than Velor," Sheela noted.

"That suits not our purpose—without horses we are doomed." He drew the knife from his boot and gave it to her. "Await me in the main temple. I will lead them on a most merry chase till nightfall."

"But if you are caught?"

"Then you must escape alone, when the skull-headed warriors make their appearance." Before she could protest, he flashed a roguish grin and leaped to the ground. He ran to the courtyard wall, scaled it with pantherish ease and stood, fists on hips, watching the quarreling band who were too intent upon themselves to take notice of him.

"Do you seek me, Velor?" Alon called tauntingly.

The group abruptly fell silent and looked toward the intruder. Drawing his sword, Velor stepped from the group and scowled up at Alon. "So there you are, you would-be usurper!" He motioned to the men. "Take him!" To his further rage, Alon disappeared from atop the wall in a backward somersault as a howl went up and several arrows whistled toward him. "After him, louts!" Velor roared, and the courtyard became a scene of frantic activity.

Sheela watched while Alon led the angry men away on a frustrating chase through the ruins. Then she left the roof and stole to the main temple. She was making her way across a chamber adjoining the altar room when, with shocking swiftness, the apparently solid stone floor fell beneath her feet. Her startled cry was cut short as she crashed down onto a brittle, uneven flooring that gave beneath her weight, raising a huge, billowing cloud of dust, and blackness descended upon her.

After a wild pursuit through various apartments of the main palace, Alon found he was trapped in a dead end corridor. Placing his back against the wall, he kept the men at bay with his slashing sword, until archers arrived and compelled his surrender. He was then marched outside to meet his fate.

Sheela awoke to find the air stifling with dust and decay. She sat up and was horrified to see that she lay atop the headless warriors' rotting corpses, which filled the large room. Fighting back sickness and panic, she looked up at the fading sunlight, spilling in from a window in the room above, illuminating the rectangular opening fifteen feet above her.

One of the hinges had come loose with age, and her weight had caused the trap door to give way, hanging precariously by the remaining hinge. She tried standing on a stack of bodies, but they crumbled beneath her booted feet.

Though she had lost her knife in the fall, Sheela found a long two-handed sword among the grisly, mummified remains, and, by the rust-colored stains, guessed that it had been used to execute the victims. A desperate plan came to her. She tore her cape into long strips, knotted them together into a rope, then tied one end around the middle of the sword, and threw it up at one corner of the opening.

It was a tiresome process; with every miss she courted decapitation, as the large sword fell back at her. Finally, she succeeded in positioning it diagonally across the corner, and carefully began climbing up the makeshift rope.

The sun had given way to the moon by the time she dragged herself over the top and lay gasping and shuddering at her harrowing experience. As she rose to leave, there was a faint rustling from below. She turned. Nothing was climbing out of the pit, and there was only empty silence. Sheela whirled and fled from the temple on winged feet.

Once outside, the cool air helped calm her overwrought senses. She heard men's boisterous voices coming from a nearby area and, fearing for Alon, went to investigate.

The bandits were camped in the wide, once-splendid courtyard of the main palace. Slipping off her boots, she crept forward, crouched in the shadows of a fallen statue and surveyed the camp. She tensed on seeing Alon's securely trussed form lying near one of the cooking fires. The red-bearded giant walked up, nudged him with a booted foot, none too gently, but he was apparently unconscious. Velor shook his shaggy head and walked away muttering disgustedly.

Though Alon had said to leave without him, Sheela's sense of honor impelled her to stay. It would mean great risk, but she must attempt to free him when the skull-headed warriors came for the men. So intent was she upon her plan, that she failed to hear the slight movement behind her until it was too late.

A pair of brawny arms encircled her torso, lifted her to her feet, and a deep voice cried:

"Velor, I've found the wench!"

Leaving their fires, the men rushed across the courtyard as Sheela and her captor fell over the statue and sprawled to the ground, struggling fiercely. She managed to twist free from her assailant and scramble to her feet, but the others were upon her.

Laughing uproariously, Velor stood back and cheered his men on as they were astonished to find they had a tremendous fight on their hands. The tall Thorgon girl lashed out furiously at the surging tide of bodies that engulfed her. She bit, kicked, punched, and raked faces open with her long nails; it was a brave but hopeless battle. Finally overcome by sheer numbers, she was dragged to the ground, held by a multitude of hands, and tightly bound hand and foot. Then the men were pulled away and Velor stood grinning down at her struggling, near-naked form, bathed in the bright moonlight.

"The mercenary said a building had fallen on you." His grin widened, showing large yellow teeth. "But he's such a liar. I said sooner or later you'd try to rescue him." He leaned closer. "Tell me, where have you been hiding all this time?" The pale-haired captive glared up at him sullenly. "Aw, don't be unfriendly to old Velor, my pretty," he cajoled, chucking her under her chin.

Sheela was tempted not to reply. Then a bold scheme came to her. If she could lure the men into the temple their destruction would be complete; and, as there was no honor in killing the helpless, she and Alon would be safe from the warriors. Perhaps they would be able to loose themselves during the battle and still escape. Lowering her eyes demurely, she answered in her most maidenly voice. "I was in the temple . . . praying to the gods for deliverance."

The despoiler of women and defiler of temples laughed loudly; the others joined in. Then he scooped Sheela up into his brawny arms. "Let us find this temple and pay homage." He glanced back at Alon. "Bring the mercenary along. We may also offer up a human sacrifice!"

Her wrists and ankles stringently tied at either end of the altar and fastened to ring bolts set in the floor, Sheela lay tautly stretched on her back staring up at the broken idols, their ghastly faces made even more grotesque by the flickering torchlight. Four men stood holding torches and chanting off-key while Velor conducted a mock ceremony, anointing her naked body with wine. The lukewarm red liquid ran down Sheela's glistening form and blended with the dark crimson stain on the cold stone beneath her. Then, as Alon, lashed to a nearby pillar, and the others watched, the hulking bandit chief drained the remaining wine, discarded the flask and clambered atop the altar and straddled her thighs. His grin wilted as he read the icy contempt and promise of deadly retribution flashing in his captive's large amber eyes.

Abruptly the chanting stopped and a stunned silence fell over the room. Turning his head, Velor saw the men frozen like statues, then followed their gaze and gaped uncomprehendingly at the skull-headed warriors pouring out of an adjoining room in unceasing numbers.

As the men stood transfixed, the warriors, twin flames dancing inside their eye sockets, marched across the vast room in a solemn procession. A wine jug shattered, spreading its red contents across the floor, and its resounding crash galvanized the men into action. Some fled screaming, others stood rooted in fear, babbling, whimpering, praying to gods they had neglected for years, while the remaining men drew their weapons and prepared to meet the charging warriors.

Leaping to the floor Velor grabbed his sword from beside the altar, bellowed a fierce battle cry and sailed into the melee, savagely rending bodies in twain, and sending naked skulls sailing about the room.

Frantically fighting her ropes, Sheela

writhed upon the altar as the battle raged around her. Her plan would be in vain unless she and Alon freed themselves. A glance at him told her that she could expect no help; he was even more stringently tied. A wild sword stroke sliced the rope connecting her firmly bound wrists to the ring bolt and she sat up, hastily working at the tight knots with her teeth. Finally, the rope reluctantly parted. She quickly untied her ankles and rolled off the altar as a bandit and a skull warrior fell onto it, locked in deadly combat.

Snatching a fallen torch, Sheela burned her way to Alon, but Velor rushed up before she could free him. She stood protectively in front of Alon and brandished the flame. The red-bearded giant easily swatted it from her hand with a flick of his blade, then threateningly advanced, backing her against Alon and the pillar. As Velor raised his arm, desire for life forced Sheela to change her original plan.

"Only *I* can rid you of the skull-headed warriors. Harm either of us and you are doomed!"

Velor glared murderously. "You knowingly brought us to this ruin?"

She nodded and smiled mirthlessly. "And my price to end it, is our freedom!" The bandit chief bristled, glancing about at his rapidly falling men and the warriors blocking the exits. "Quickly, your answer!"

The red-bearded bandit reluctantly lowered his sword. "Agreed, you sorcerous wench!"

"Trust him not!" Alon warned.

"I'll stand by my word," Velor growled. "But I'll not be played false!" As though for emphasis, he savagely beheaded two attacking warriors with a single stroke.

"You shan't," Sheela promised. "Now rally your men and gather torches." Velor hastened away, and Sheela told Alon of the warriors' burial room while she quickly freed him from the pillar. Then she bent and picked up her still-burning torch.

Velor banded his remaining men around Sheela, Alon and several others who also held torches, then they made a mad rush for the adjoining room. Though their numbers dwindled along the way, the group hacked a path through the sea of warriors and gained entry to the room.

More warriors urgently intercepted the group as they neared the trap door, and the fighting became even more intense. Aware of their intent, the skull warriors sought to reach those with torches. Soon only Alon and Sheela held torches. Then a warrior sliced the flaming tip from his, leaving her to accomplish the deed. Alon grabbed a dying man's sword and joined in the carnage.

Onward they pressed, with Velor's men dropping one after another. Finally naught but Alon and Velor, their long blades striking down all that came within reach, stood between Sheela and the warriors. As the things closed on them she desperately hurled her torch over their heads. Several warriors leaped up, swords wildly attempting to bat the flame from the air as it arched toward the opening in the floor.

The torch landed at the edge of the trap door, balanced for a heart-stopping moment, then tumbled down before a running warrior could reach it. He was instantly incinerated as a gigantic, fiery tongue sprung from the opening with a startling *whoosh* and scorched the high ceiling. The room echoed with a sepulchral chorus of anguished screams and the terrifying long-dead warriors began rapidly fading into thin air.

As the fire and hideous screams lessened, Sheela and the two men moved forward and stood looking down at the writhing, crackling mass of flaming corpses, then hastily retreated as a thick black cloud of foul-smelling smoke assailed them.

Pausing beside the altar to collect her clothing, Sheela followed Alon and Velor out of the temple. She hurriedly dressed while they stood deeply breathing in the fresh night air to clear the stench from their nostrils. No sooner had she completed dressing than Velor whirled on her, scowling.

"Witch of Hades. You wrought this havoc upon me!"

"Hold your tongue, ignorant clod!" Alon shouted, stepping between them, his sword at the ready. "Have you never heard of the lost city of Baalshazzar and its curse?"

The bandit's ugly face screwed up in thought. It appeared a most arduous process. Then, most slowly, his face shone with awe. "You mean this be it?"

"You are most astute, my friend."

The big man squinted at Sheela. "Then you be no witch?"

"I am a mere woman," she replied, staring back at him with large innocent eyes.

"Well now, fancy that . . ." Velor shook his mangy head and grinned. "You were jesting with me all this time." He threw back his head and laughed uproariously. But Sheela sensed there was scant mirth behind his laughter.

The three set off along the silent street to the courtyard of the main palace.

After retrieving her boots, Sheela joined Alon in the courtyard and helped him gather and load sacks of provisions onto two horses. She uncomfortably noticed Velor, who was content to lounge before a dying campfire, eying her in deep thought as he drank most crudely from a wine flask. When their task was done, Alon turned to the sullen giant.

"We now take our leave of you, swillbelly."

The redbeard took a last messy gulp, discarded the flask and lurched to his feet. He grinned cruelly. "You will go nowhere, mercenary." He drew his sword with a loud rasp that wickedly cut the silence enveloping the moonlit courtyard. "After I've settled with you, I'm taking the wench back to my camp."

Alon smiled dangerously as the brawny giant lumbered forward. "So that's how it is to be, eh?" He drew his sword and started toward Velor.

Sheela quickly sprung between the men and addressed the bandit. "You gave your word in the temple!"

He dismissed her words with a wave of his huge hand. "That was when I thought you a sorceress. Now out of the way, woman, whilst I—" He broke off as the horses suddenly shied, nervously whinnying and stamping the ground.

Their quarrel momentarily forgotten, Sheela and the men tensed, listening and straining to peer into the darkness. Numerous light footfalls were heard. Then their eyes detected the outlines of many figures, armed with bows and arrows, stealthily approaching across the dark courtyard. Velor groaned, muttered an oath, then whirled and pointed an accusing finger at Sheela.

"You did not do your job properly!" he roared. "The skull warriors still live!"

Chapter Seven

A figure in a black hooded cape boldly strode ahead of the armed group, stopped outside the edge of light cast by a dwindling campfire and stood silently regarding the three.

Looking from the figure to Sheela, Alon whispered, "There are no flames for eyes— these are not the skull warriors.".

Slowly the figure pushed back the hood, threw open the cape and stood, legs apart, hands on hips. The moonlight revealed a woman, her tall, slender, graceful body attired in two brief strips of black leather, about her firm breasts and slender hips, long matching gloves, high-heeled boots and a narrow sword belt; a gold armlet and matching ornate necklace gleamed as she stepped into the firelight.

Sheela recognized her and gave a surprised gasp. "Sumara!"

Velor turned his wrath upon the intruder. "What do you want here, Sumara!"

"*Princess* Sumara," she replied coolly.

"Bah!"

Sumara languidly eyed the three and purred, "I come to reclaim an escaped female slave, only to find that I now have two male slaves as well."

"*What*?" the bandit chief bellowed, raising his sword. "Be gone, foul wench, or I'll have your head!"

She dismissed him with an amused smile. "Save your threats for children and old ones, Velor, and lay down your sword before my archers loose their arrows."

Sword raised, the redbeard hesitated, scanning the large group in the surrounding blackness, their bows drawn taut, arrows poised to fly at him. His face mirrored his strain as he sought to reach a decision; it was most obvious that he did not relish surrender.

Seeing the hopelessness of their situation, Alon tossed his sword to the ground and looked to Velor. "Go on, dolt," he taunted, "let them save me the bother of killing you."

"You'd like that, wouldn't you?" the giant sneered. Alon grinned in reply. As though to spite him, Velor hurled his sword to the ground. It clanged loudly on the broken marble walkway.

Sumara smiled triumphantly and, casually motioning with one gloved hand, called, "Bind them and place them on their horses." Instantly, several women left the group and hurried toward the prisoners. Zambra moved to Sumara's side and stood watching coldly, her eyes solely upon Sheela.

The journey back was equally arduous. The merciless sun turned the unshaded land into a blazing furnace, filling the sky and sand with its flaming glare. Beneath the cape that had been loosely draped about her shoulders, Sheela felt the perspiration streaming over the curves of her body instantly evaporating as the heat remorselessly sucked the life juices from her. As before, when she had lain helpless beside the stream, the rawhide bonds added to her discomfort. The sun's glare became steadily stronger. Though she narrowed her large eyes to slits, the glare was still most painful, and she became convinced the sun had but one intent: to add her bones to this barren inhospitable land.

Finally the group sought refuge from the full strength of the noon sun in the blessed shade of a hillside. There they rested until the naked sun was well past its zenith before resuming their trek. Still, the terrifying oven-heat continued to bake the land. As the dunes and hills became more numerous, the riders veered from their straight line of march and traveled in their shadows as much as possible.

It was late in the day, and the sun's fury had at last waned. The riders had no difficulty keeping in the long dark shadows that stretched across the sands from the towering mountain ranges. With the coolness of day, lagging energies returned and, except for the three captives, spirits rose.

And it was then that they happened to encounter a large patrol of the king's soldiers.

It was too late to run and there was no place to hide in the wide open stretch of sand between the surrounding mountains. The group halted, watching the soldiers gallop from behind a hill and spread out, blocking their way.

"We are greatly outnumbered," Zambra announced grimly.

Sumara smiled and shook her raven head. "The king's soldiers fight badly. We will break through their ranks." She drew her sword and nudged her horse forward. Drawing their weapons, Zambra and the others followed, spreading out to meet the charging soldiers.

A great din rent the air as the two groups collided savagely. Steel clashed upon steel, men and women died screaming, heads and limbs were severed, cloven skulls and slit stomachs added their gory contents to the blood-soaked earth.

A whistling blow from a broad, straight sword decapitated the woman leading Sheela's mount. A red geyser spewed high into the air, bathing the surrounding combatants, as the horse moved through the press with its headless rider.

His eyes wild with battle-lust, the soldier raised his bloody sword for a cut at Sheela, who watched in helpless terror. But before the death stroke could be completed, an arrow tore into his armpit and sent the soldier toppling to the ground, where he lay writhing and screaming until Sheela's wildly rearing horse dashed out his brains with his hooves.

With her arms and wrists tightly lashed behind her and her ankles connected under the horse by rawhide bonds, Sheela frantically knee-gripped the frightened animal, to keep from falling to her own death beneath its hoofs. Screaming shrilly and striking out at those about it, the horse reared in one direction, then another, seeking escape from the surrounding clangor of battle and smell of fresh blood. The cape slipped from Sheela's shoulders and nigh became entangled in the animal's legs, as its hoofs stamped it deeply into the sand.

Sheela desperately looked about for aid, but the participants were far too busily engaged in the slaughter to take heed of her distress. She saw Zambra in the midst of the fight, laughing joyfully as her blade laid open a man's face. As her horse wheeled, Sheela then saw a band of women who had won free of the crush spin around on the backs of their galloping mounts to face the pursuing soldiers and unleash their bows with deadly accuracy. She caught sight of Sumara, on foot, defending herself with sword and dirk, slashing her way toward her.

Leaving her dirk lodged in a soldier's rent corselet, Sumara caught the loose reins in her free hand and, avoiding the crimson-covered hoofs, brought Sheela's terrified horse under control. She swung easily up behind her, urged the horse forward, and cleared a wide, bloody swath with her flailing sword. They broke through the ragged ranks, leaving a score of dead and dying in their wake, and galloped toward a yawning canyon, with half a dozen soldiers in mad pursuit.

The women raced into the canyon well ahead of their pursuers, and Sumara turned the horse into one of the numerous narrow defiles. Halting around the bend, she quickly gagged her captive with a long strip torn from her tattered, blood-stained cape, then dismounted and held the horse's muzzle as the soldiers were heard entering the canyon. The sounds grew louder. She pressed back against the steep wall and spoke to the animal in low, soothing tones. The soldiers galloped past and continued along the main canyon. When their hoofbeats had faded into the distance, she again mounted and guided the weary, wheezing horse up a path between the towering masses of stone. Only after they were well away from the main canyon and high up into the rocks did she loosen Sheela's gag and draw the cloth down about her neck.

The passage continued to narrow as it rose higher, and the women's legs came nigh to being bruised by the rocks on either side of the trail. Then it abruptly emerged out onto a wider mountain trail. As they began following the new trail, the women heard a curious drumming sound, resembling a hive of monstrous, restless bees. The trail descended between winged pinnacles of rock, to a barren valley encircled by violent flame-red mountains. The drumming sound echoed through the valley as heaps of reddish sand shifted across the mountains' rock faces. Sumara halted the horse and solemnly studied the valley for a long moment; then she said wryly:

"The gods continue to have sport with me."

Craning her neck, Sheela glanced back at her curiously. "What do you mean?"

"This is the Valley of Death and Madness. It is said that those who spend the night here either die, or are driven mad by dead spirits who turn into wolfmen and other cursed creatures."

Noting the gravity in Sumara's beautiful face, Sheela turned back and stared apprehensively at the valley. As though seeking to heighten their foreboding, the drumming sound continued to echo through the valley as the wind shifted the sand against the smooth rock faces. Then Sumara spoke, her voice heavy with resignation.

"The soldiers will not risk entering, so we have no choice but to take refuge inside."

Sheela remained silent; as a captive her word mattered naught; besides, she had no better suggestion to offer. She hoped it was but a fanciful tale for gullible minds. Still, the encounter with the skull-headed warriors was fresh in her memory, and it was most unsettling. Then her thoughts were disrupted by the horse's forward movement, and they entered the valley.

The setting sun cast immense, grotesque shadows across the valley floor, as Sumara and Sheela rode toward a large grouping of flame-colored rocks rising up on one side of the valley. Sumara guided the weary, stumbling horse high up into the rocks, so that they were afforded a view of both the valley floor and the trail beyond, and then camped beside a cascading rivulet of distasteful, but drinkable red water.

After drinking their fill, Sumara pulled Sheela to her feet and led her to some nearby rocks, where she roughly sat her down with her back against a large rock. Sheela watched impassively while she used two long thongs to deftly bind her legs and ankles, completing her helplessness. The princess sat back and eyed her prisoner with a pleased smile.

"This will insure that I am able to give my full attention to whatever dangers may appear this night."

"But we should face them together," Sheela said, writhing uncomfortably, "and I am of no help like this."

Sumara patted her sword hilt. "My sword is all the help I need." She smiled mockingly. "Besides, you are the one who refuses to fight."

The Thorgon girl met her eyes coolly. "I'll fight to protect my life—but not to help you usurp a throne."

"I am no usurper!" Sumara flared. "The throne is mine by birthright. I am King Jator's half-sister. And, being one week older, I am the rightful ruler of Istwar!"

"Then why are you not ruler?"

Sumara's exquisite face hardened. "From childhood Jator and I have hated each other, and upon our father's death he usurped my throne. Instead of death or banishment, he delighted in making me his concubine, and forced me to perform degrading acts, not only with him, but the court nobility and male and female slaves, during the almost nightly palace orgies." She broke off and looked away, bitter and shamed.

As Sheela silently waited for Sumara to continue, she could not help comparing

Sumara's sufferings to what her own fate would have been under the Rhobians. That empathy somewhat softened her animosity toward the beautiful, haughty princess.

The drumming sound echoed through the valley, rousing Sumara from her private thoughts. She looked back at Sheela and resumed her tale.

"Through bribery I escaped, accompanied by some slave girls and a small group of the palace guards. Then I established my own camp, where women are supreme."

"What of the palace guards?"

"They are now my slaves. You most probably saw some of them while you were in my camp."

Sheela leaned forward, her amber eyes wide with indignation. "They aided you— and you rewarded them with slavery!"

Sumara nodded, amused at her reaction. "And after I regain my throne, I will extend my policy of female supremacy over the entire country."

For a moment, Sheela could only stare at her. Then, fighting back her outrage, she remembered her father's words on ruling and made an earnest attempt to enlighten the princess. "A good queen is concerned with the welfare of *all* her subjects." Sumara tensed, her blue eyes narrowing. Stubbornly refusing to heed caution, Sheela took petty delight in adding, "It appears as if the people of Istwar will be worse off than they are under King Jator."

Sumara furiously backhanded Sheela across her mouth with a black gloved hand, almost knocking her over. "You dare to lecture me on ruling, you stupid North Land barbarian wench!"

Her face smarting mightily, Sheela dazedly raised her head and, ignoring the thin trickle of blood oozing from one corner of her mouth, glared hatefully at her tormentor. She opened her mouth to speak, but the princess quickly leaned forward, yanked up the loose strip of cloth hanging about her neck and forced it between her teeth. Before her tongue could dislodge the cloth, Sumara drew the knot tight at the back of her head, firmly holding the stifling gag in place.

"That will still your insolent mouth!" Sumara said haughtily, as she stood and glared down at Sheela, who angrily shook her head, vainly attempting to rid the cloth from her mouth. Sumara turned on her heel and arrogantly stalked away, leaving her struggling captive glowering after her.

With the coming of night the wind lessened, and only an occasional drumming resounded through the silent valley. A full moon shone down on the valley, whose floor was shrouded by a strange mist. Sheela slept fitfully, waking and shifting about, uncomfortable with her gag and bonds, against the hard rock. Shivering in the cool night air, she glanced over at Sumara sleeping nearby, comfortably wrapped in her cape, one gloved hand resting on the hilt of her sword, lying beside her. Sheela eyed her vehemently and imagined revenge most foul. Then the horse's nervous movements intruded upon her thoughts.

Sumara was instantly awake, her hand gripping her sword. Her eyes went first to Sheela, who sat staring back at her, wide-eyed over her gag, then darted to the horse, snorting and moving about uneasily near the pool of water. The swirling mist revealed only the frightened animal.

The women remained motionless, listening keenly as their eyes roamed the misty clearing. Then the faint sounds of someone skulking in the rocks above reached their ears. Sheela leaned forward, her large eyes imploring Sumara to free her. But the princess paid her no heed.

Sliding her blade from its scabbard, Sumara slipped off her cape and silently eased herself to her feet. Sheela urgently squirmed forward, emitting low incoherent sounds behind her gag. Sumara shot her a stern glance and put a black gloved finger to her lips, then, crouching low, stole into the mist.

Tugging futilely at her bonds, Sheela apprehensively watched Sumara's figure stealthily slip to the rocks on the other side of the small clearing, and begin climbing up toward the sounds. Her nerves tight as bow strings, she sat rigid with expectation. Was some supernatural beast lurking atop the rocks, ready to pounce down upon Sumara and rend her limb from limb? Under other circumstances she would relish such an occurrence, but trussed and helpless, her fate was in Sumara's hands. Through the parting mist, she saw Sumara quietly working her way toward the top—and then it happened.

Framed in the moonlight, a towering shape loomed against the sky and, with a roar, sprung down at Sumara.

Abruptly, clouds hid the moon, and Sheela saw only two dark forms fall through the mist and slam to the ground. The indistinguishable shapes rolled about, struggling furiously in the dark shadows. Then the hulking figure struck Sumara mightily upon her jaw, and she lay still.

Urgently jerking at her bonds, her eyes large and fearful, Sheela watched as the massive form rose and lumbered toward her through the mist, waving its arms and roaring, beastlike. She recoiled against the rock and froze, vainly willing herself invisible as the dark shambling outline drew nearer . . . nearer . . .

The roars abruptly became lusty laughter, and the dark clouds withdrew from the moon, to reveal Velor's grinning face. Recognizing him, Sheela gaped in surprise. Doubled over with laughter Velor stumbled up and plopped down beside her as she regained her composure and sat seething.

"Scared you good, didn't I, girl?" he said, slapping her thigh and squeezing it good-naturedly. Sheela did her best to kill him with a withering glare. Unfortunately, she was no witch. The redbeard only grinned. "You do not look happy to see me." Were she not gagged she would have singed his ears with her reply. Reluctantly removing his coarse hand from her smooth thigh, the giant fumbled with the knot holding the cloth over her mouth. She winced as his clumsy fingers also pulled at strands of her long white-golden hair. He drew the cloth from her mouth and sat back, pleased.

Sheela drew a relieved breath and fixed her cool amber eyes upon him. "How did you find us, Velor?"

"During the fight with the soldiers, I broke my bonds." He grinned and flexed his muscular arms. Sheela's icy expression told him that she was not impressed. He continued his tale. "I then followed your trail. The soldiers who pursued you are now food for the buzzards." He loudly cracked his knuckles for emphasis and began untying the long thongs about her arms and body.

"What of Alon?" Sheela asked anxiously.

The burly bandit scowled. "I know naught of his fate—and care less!" He removed the thongs from her body and turned his attention to the one about her legs.

"Velor, my wrists?" Sheela said, holding her bound hands out to one side of her slim body.

"You'll stay like you are until we reach my camp." He pulled the thong free from her legs, but left her ankles tied.

"What do you intend?" Sheela asked suspiciously.

Velor grinned and chucked her under her chin. "You're to become my most favored love slave." Sheela jerked her head away and again tried in vain to destroy him with a look. Velor only picked up the thongs and stood. "Now I must put these on Sumara, who will become a mere kitchen slave." He turned and ambled off into the churning fog.

Squinting into the mist, Sheela saw Velor kneel beside Sumara's still form and set about binding her. She desperately glanced about in search of some sharp object to cut her bonds with, but, as previously, nothing availed itself. Then she heard a loud beastly growl echo through the rocks, and her spine tingled. She jerked her head around and looked to Velor.

The red-bearded giant had paused in his work and was staring out at the surrounding mist and blackness. Nothing was seen, and there was only an ominous silence. He hurriedly completed his task, then picked up Sumara's sword and turned toward Sheela. But a nearby savage growl caused him to whirl around, sword raised, ready to strike.

Then, slowly, a wolfman emerged from the dank fog.

Her heart thudding, Sheela sat staring in disbelief at the shaggy man-beast walking on two legs. She saw Velor also gape for a moment. Then he answered the growls with a fierce battle cry and hurled himself at the creature.

As the sword struck the beast there was a blinding explosion of light. Velor bellowed as the sword glowed in his hand, as bright as steel newly removed from a blacksmith's forge. The giant was hurled to the ground, and the wolfman abruptly vanished. Slowly the glow faded from the sword in Velor's limp hand.

Sheela sat staring in wide-eyed confusion. Then a wolf's howl, from another part of the clearing, gripped her in an icy fear. Stiffly her head turned in that direction.

Two wolfmen slowly approached through the swirling mist.

Mesmerized by terror, Sheela stared frozenly.

Growling savagely, the shaggy creatures shambled toward her. As they drew nearer, slaver was seen dripping from their jaws and their fangs gleamed wickedly in the moonlight.

The blood ran cold in Sheela's veins, chilling her whole body. Raw fear constricted her throat, stifling her scream. Her body trembling uncontrollably, her head moving jerkily from side to side, she helplessly watched the man-beasts close upon her. Their stench overwhelmed her senses. She could feel their foul breath upon her near-naked body. Their red eyes glowed eerily through the mist like the pits of Hell. They were almost before her. She watched, trance-like, all thought of useless struggle gone. She could do naught but await their cold fangs upon her throat.

Suddenly a tall, gaunt figure in a black hooded robe appeared between Sheela and the wolfmen, who stopped and stood growling viciously. Arms outstretched at his sides, the figure blocked the creatures' path, and his mere presence seemed to hold them at bay. But for how long? Her long legs drawn up to her body, Sheela sat hunched against the rock and stared up at the figure's back as her fear-numbed brain sought to give words to her thoughts. Then a familiar calm, forceful voice penetrated her fear, both startling her and bringing reassurance.

"Clear your mind of all thought, my queen."

"Tokar!"

The wolfmen edged closer, growling menacingly.

"Hurry. Obey me!" Tokar urgently commanded.

With great difficulty, Sheela closed her eyes and concentrated on making her mind a blank. The beastly growls began to lose their intensity. Hesitantly parting her long lashes, she was surprised to see the two wolfmen's forms flicker and slowly fade into the mist. Though they appeared to be gone, she carefully kept her mind a void. The old man turned and looked down at her.

"They are gone."

Somehow Sheela found her voice. "What made them leave?"

The witch-man smiled. "You did."

She shook her head, greatly confused. "But how?"

"The wolfmen are thought-forms of supernatural beings, which are falsely created by people's superstitions that this valley is haunted. They obtain their form from the thought-force energy of their creators who, this time, were you and Velor, because of his little jest with you."

"Then I shall think no more of them." She squirmed and smiled imploringly. "Now please untie me, dearest friend."

He shrugged regretfully. "I am most sorry, my queen, but I cannot do so."

She frowned and wriggled impatiently. "Must I command you?"

The witch-man shook his head. "It would do no good. I am here before you in my mind body form." Noting her bewilderment, he smiled and paced about before her, turning around in a complete circle.

"Have you not noticed the difference in my appearance?"

For a moment Sheela could only gape. Then she replied in awe, "You move freely without a staff . . . and there is no deformity . . ."

The old man beamed and said proudly, "I am presently the equal of any Thorgon in appearance."

Sheela nodded and said most sincerely, "You have always been that in my eyes, dear Tokar."

He was clearly both pleased and touched by her compliment. Then he waved a pale hand in dismissal. "Enough of me. I have had counsel with Lanzad."

Sheela could not keep the disdain from her voice. "And what of worth does that lustful demon have to say?"

Tokar's face became grave. "You will not like it, but you must hear me out." Sheela eyed him warily. Tokar hesitated, then drew a deep breath. "Princess Sumara is important to your cause—and you must aid her against King Jator."

Sheela was stunned into speechlessness. Then she exploded wrathfully. "I will do no such thing. The bitch has done naught but torment me since we met. I sit before you, bound by her own hands!"

Tokar fixed her with an earnest gaze. "Sumara will change. She will be a good queen—and a helpful ally—once she is made to realize that her power lies with her people." Sheela snorted and sought to protest, but he pressed on. "There is a man named Korr who is greatly admired by the people. He will help her. You are to convince her to go among the people, and he will contact her."

"How am I to do that?" demanded Sheela. "She regards me as not only her slave, but a stupid, North Land barbarian!"

"Surely a woman knows best how to deal with another woman." His words brought only a disgusted sigh from his beautiful queen, who fidgeted and glanced toward Sumara's still form. Tokar followed her gaze, then looked down at her and cleared his throat diplomatically. "There is one more thing you must do." Sheela eyed him narrowly, waiting for him to continue. Braving her wrath, Tokar said, "Velor is also important to Sumara's success, and you must see that they join forces."

Sheela made no attempt to conceal her outrage. "Now you ask too much! That brutish oaf lusts for me and plans to make me his love slave." She jerked at the long thong imprisoning her slender wrists. "Were I free,

181

I would gladly throttle both of them!"

"You must cast aside your animosities," spoke the old man soothingly. "Remember what is asked of you is for the good of our own people."

The young queen heaved an aggravated sigh and made a most tremendous effort to allow logic to intervene over prejudice. It was not an easy task. "And how do my people fare under the Rhobians?" she asked.

"Resistance is rampant. The Rhobians have yet to solidify their hold upon the land."

"At least, you have brought me one bit of welcome news," Sheela said testily.

"Alas, I wish that I could report the Rhobians have been driven from our land."

"I, too," the pale-haired Thorgon girl said quietly. "My heart aches most fiercely to see my homeland once more."

The old man nodded, his gray eyes compassionate. "I understand, my queen."

Thoughts of home came flooding back to Sheela, and her acute loneliness brought tears to her eyes. She looked away, fearing that Tokar would see them. It was not right that a subject—even a beloved one as Tokar—should see a queen's tears. Then his words brought her attention quickly back to him.

"I can remain no longer, my queen."

Her eyes widened in surprise as his body slowly became semitransparent. She urgently leaned toward him as the mist threatened to totally obscure his form from her eyes. "Please, Tokar," she cried, "stay and aid me!"

Only the old man's gray shaggy head remained visible. "My energy is waning." The disembodied head smiled. Though Tokar was a beloved friend, the sight of a floating head was somewhat disconcerting to Sheela. "Farewell, my queen," he said, his voice becoming faint. "I am certain that you will prevail." Then the head was gone.

"Tokar!" Sheela called into the mist. But there was no reply. She waited, desperately hoping he would reappear. Her hopes were for naught. She sighed and sat sulkily pondering her dilemma. She tried to content herself with the rationalization that a queen must oft make great sacrifices for her people. But it was not a completely comforting thought. Scowling her irritation, she looked toward Sumara and Velor and was much relieved to see both were still unconscious. But how long would they remain in that placid state? She knew she must free herself before they awakened, if she was to accomplish the most difficult and unpleasant task Tokar had demanded of her. An attempt to slip her wrists from her bonds confirmed that the entwined leather thong was still stubbornly unyielding.

Across the clearing something shone in the moonlight. It was Sumara's sword, laying in Velor's limp, open palm.

Sheela eyed the glittering sword thoughtfully. It was the answer to her prayers. But, as she had not the power to move objects, she must somehow go to it. A most simple matter—were she not bound hand and foot. She judged the distance to be no more than six dozen lengthy strides. It may as well be six dozen leagues. Regardless, she must reach it.

Clearing the negativity from her mind, Sheela deliberated over her mode of travel. None were very appealing, and all were very demeaning to a queen's dignity. She quickly discarded the thought of trying to gain her feet and hopping; a fall could be quite disastrous. To roll her body over and over in the dirt, like a log, would be exceedingly messy and dirty work. Squirming, crablike, on her side was equally offensive. There was but one way left to her. She took a deep breath, extended her long legs before her and dug her high heels into the dirt.

Pulling with her heels, raising her firm buttocks, and pushing with her bound hands, Sheela began worming her way across the clearing.

It was a slow, painful, and most arduous task.

Chapter Eight

As the first light of dawn brightened the gray-black sky, Sheela sat carefully sawing the long thong about her nerveless wrists against the sword that she had (with much trouble) thrust deeply into the ground, its hilt braced between two rocks. It was patient, demanding work; and patience was one of her far lesser virtues. The threat that Velor might awaken at any second did naught to instill that virtue. But the knowledge that the loss of circulation had deadened all feeling in her hands and if they slipped she could be unknowingly slicing her wrists open to the bone did much to still her impatience.

A low moan interrupted her intense concentration.

Sheela tensed, her eyes darting to Velor. The red-bearded giant lay sprawled on his back, silent and unmoving. The moan was heard again. She shifted her eyes to Sumara.

Body tautly bowed, the raven-haired princess lay upon her stomach. Her gloved wrists and arms were bound together behind her back and joined to her booted ankles by a short length of thong. Velor had done his work well; she looked most uncomfortable. Sheela could almost kiss him. The princess stirred as consciousness returned and gave a start at discovering she was bound. Her confusion became anger as she struggled for naught. She turned her head and looked about to see her captive, still bound, now sitting on the other side of the clearing. Her face expressing her dismay, she asked harshly, "Who has done this?"

"See for yourself," Sheela replied, nodding toward Velor and resuming to rub her bonds against the sword edge.

Sumara shifted about, stared in surprise at his unconscious body, then looked back at her. "Is he dead?"

The Thorgon girl shook her head. "Merely resting." The severed thong fell from her wrists. She brought her nerveless hands before her and let them fall limply onto her lap. She was much relieved to see that her long slender fingers were not swollen, though they had felt as large as sausages while she had been at work on her bonds. She willed them to move and pain, most excruciating, needled through her hands as circulation slowly returned. Sumara's urgent voice diverted her mind from her torment.

"Hurry, we must be free before he awakens!"

"*We?*"

Sumara's blue eyes widened in frank surprise. "You would leave me here with him?"

"Gladly." Smiling at the thought, Sheela drew her legs up to her body, leaned over and began plucking at the tight knots confining her booted ankles.

"You foul, miserable barbarian!" Sumara cried, thrashing in her bonds. She quickly realized the futility and allowed her rage to cool. "Free me and I will aid you against the Rhobians," she said craftily.

The Thorgon girl paused and looked up from the obstinate knots. "Even if you were to keep your word, it is worthless. You have no hope of defeating King Jator, as the people are not with you, and you have no allies— not even Velor and his bandits."

"I need no one!"

Sheela smiled innocently. "At this moment, you do need me." The beautiful, imperious princess scowled, but made no reply. Sheela gloated inwardly. Tokar had denied her the revenge she sought, so she must derive what pleasures, however scant, she could from this most welcome change in their fortunes. She gave the knots her attention and said disinterestedly, "If things were different, and I knew you had hope of regaining your throne, I would do all to aid you."

"Then I will make allies," Sumara agreed, far too quickly. "Now free me."

Sheela untangled the rawhide thong from her ankles and grimaced as, again, full circulation begrudgingly returned. Then she solemnly eyed Sumara. "You must give me your *royal* word that I am no longer your slave, and you will treat me with the proper respect one royal personage shows another."

As she had hoped, Sumara's royal word was most precious to her, for she hesitated and her face made no secret of her disdain. Then wisdom prevailed, though her voice was sullen. "You have my royal word . . . *Queen* Sheela."

Sheela stood and stamped her feet to aid her circulation. "You promise to meet with the people of Istwar?" Again the princess sullenly pledged her royal word. Sheela drew a deep breath and made her last demand. "And you agree to make peace with Velor and ally yourself to him?"

Sumara could no longer contain her royal temper. "That swine—I'll have none of him!"

Sheela calmly met her inexorable gaze, then shrugged indifferently and picked up the sword. "You cannot afford to fight both the king and Velor's band at once."

"That is *my* affair!"

"And I will leave you to it." Sheela turned away and marched toward the horse, standing near the pool of red water. She had taken less than a dozen strides when Sumara's desperate voice stopped her.

"Wait. I will do as you ask!"

Repressing a smile, she turned back and eyed her sternly. "Your royal word?"

The princess looked as though she had ingested a rancid meal. Her voice was scarcely audible. "My *royal* word."

Sheela heaved a huge sigh of great relief. She had accomplished the first part of this most intricate task Tokar had bestowed upon her. Would that Velor proved no more difficult. She went to Sumara and freed her.

But she kept possession of the sword.

Her long lovely legs dangling, the sword resting in her lap, Sheela sat atop a rock and watched the early morning sun climb higher above the mountain peaks as she listened absently to the monotonous droning of Velor and Sumara's haggling voices. Though their voices occasionally rose in anger, neither had yet attempted to throttle the other. Sumara had grudgingly taken her advice to win Velor over with a kind deed; and the red-bearded giant had awakened to confusedly find her bathing his face with a wet cloth torn from her cape. With admirable effort on her part, Sumara had overcome his suspicions, and Sheela had then left them to conclude their peace treaty. That had been several hours ago. She now felt a great impulse to snatch each by the hair and bang their mulish heads soundly together, until they gave in to reason. Pleasant as that thought might be, she knew she must leave them to their own devices. Their wrangling grew in intensity and she looked in alarm toward the two animated figures.

"You—a general in *my* army!" cried Sumara. Then, hands on her hips, she threw back her raven head and laughed derisively.

Cheeks almost the color of his beard, Velor thrust his face before hers. "I was a *captain* in your father's army. I know more about tactics than you or anybody else!"

"Ha!"

"That's my condition—take it or leave it!" the giant said, jutting out his jaw for emphasis.

From atop her rock Sheela held her breath, awaiting Sumara's reply. Were the matter of less importance she would have laughed aloud at the sight of two adults, their stance and behavior as ridiculous as children daring each other to cross a line drawn in the dirt. How many fights would be avoided, she wondered, if the belligerents could but stand back and view themselves with a detached air?

"Well?" the outlaw chief demanded.

Sumara became thoughtful. "You are certain that you can deliver five hundred men to me?"

He nodded his huge head. "And good fighters, every one!"

A smile slowly spread over the princess' face. "Very well, *General* Velor, bring your army to my camp before the week has ended."

The big man grinned, showing yellow teeth. "Done, Your Highness!" They clasped forearms, sealing their agreement.

After Velor had taken his leave, Sheela concealed her misgivings and returned Sumara's sword. "Rest your fears, Queen Sheela," Sumara said, buckling on her sword belt, "my royal word still stands." Her smooth brow creased, belying her words of cheer. "Now let us go in search of the nearest city or village, and I will meet with my people."

It was noon when they stopped atop a rise and spied an approaching caravan below. "We will draw less attention if we enter the city with that caravan," Sumara said. Sheela agreed, and they rode down and joined in the long procession.

The next few hours proved enlightening to both women. Sheela marveled over the splendid goods from far away lands, and listened with avid interest to the traders' tales of exotic places. But most of all, she was enthralled by the towering, spindly-legged, tawny beasts of burden bearing people and trade goods upon their huge humped backs. Though she found it hard to accept, their owners swore that the awkward beasts, called camels, could outrun the swiftest horse and go for days on end without water, even in the driest of deserts. But they also possessed a foul, balky temperament, spitting their juices upon the unwary, and so great was their dislike for man, that it was said a dying camel would walk for many leagues to an oasis and fall dead in its water, just to pollute it for man. A brief ride upon one's pitching, swaying back left her with blurred vision and churning stomach, as though she had been once more upon the Volu River's mighty rapids, and she determined that she would stay with horses.

Sumara was heartened to learn that King Jator was hated by one and all, as his caravan tariffs were double those of other rulers. She masterfully restrained her fiery temper and kept her face a void as she heard herself and her Amazons spoken of in the most derogatory terms. It was none too soon for her when they came to a small town, and she and Sheela were able to unobtrusively take their leave as the caravan moved along the winding, wide, crowded street, lined with flat-roofed, mud-and-stone dwellings.

The women left their horse and wandered through the market place, surreptitiously eavesdropping on various conversations. Besides confirming what they had already learned from the caravan, the people spoke glowingly of a man named Korr. Sheela had refrained from telling Sumara about this champion of the people. After all, how would she, a stranger in these lands, know about him; and she felt that to speak of Tokar's visit would only make Sumara believe that she was quite mad. She was pleased that Sumara's interest became more avid as they continued to hear tales of Korr's good deeds among the people.

Later Sheela stood ravenously munching on a strange, delicious, but very messy and seedy fruit known as a pomegranate, while Sumara engaged the aged proprietress of the fruit stand in conversation. She almost choked on a mouthful of seeds as the old woman's wrinkled face darkened at the mention of Sumara's name.

"She is a female jackal, preying on all!" She paused in her diatribe to spit contemptuously, her rheumy eyes narrowing in rage. "When she escaped King Jator the people cheered and were ready to join her against the tyrant. But what did she do, she made war upon her own people!"

"Perhaps she did not know that they were with her," Sumara suggested.

The old woman shrugged broadly. "She should have made an appeal to them!" Sumara fell silent, pondering her logic.

"We have heard talk of a man known as Korr," Sheela said, trying to steer the conversation onto the right course. "It is said he is a hero of the people."

The tradeswoman nodded. "He gives aid and comfort to all who ask."

"Where is this charitable man found?" Sumara asked.

"No one knows. He simply appears whenever he knows he is needed."

"How convenient," Sumara muttered dubiously.

"Have you ever had need of him?" Sheela asked.

The old woman was about to respond, but abruptly hesitated and, being a simple, straightforward peasant, was unable to hide the light of suspicion that appeared in her watery eyes. "No." Then she hastened to add, "Nor have I ever seen him." She quickly turned her attention to arranging the various fruits displayed on her stand.

Sumara broke the silence, her voice hinting of impatience. "I am curious to meet this Korr." The proprietress paid her no heed and continued busying herself with the fruit, which needed no further arranging. The princess pressed on. "I would pay for such a meeting."

"Save your money!" snapped the old crone, not looking up. "I cannot help you."

"Know you someone who can?" persisted Sumara.

The tradeswoman squinted up at the women, her lined face resolute as she shook her gray head and motioned them away with a withered claw. "Kindly move on, so that others may take your place!"

Restraining her temper, Sumara turned on her heel and strode away. Sheela followed, conscious of the old hag's eyes burning holes in her back. It was with relief that she merged into the anonymity of the crowd and was shut off from her vision.

Though Sheela was against it, Sumara insisted on trying to tempt others to take them to Korr. Her efforts met with constant rebuff.

As dusk mantled the town square, the two women sat on a ledge of the main fountain and idly watched the last of the crowd disperse for their homes or the taverns. Sumara glanced dejectedly to her companion.

"I have met with my people, and they are a surly lot."

"Only at the mention of your name," Sheela said dryly.

"I have given them little enough to praise me for," Sumara agreed. She sighed and shook her head regretfully. "Had I but known they were with me at the beginning, I might now be sitting on my throne . . ."

"It is not too late to win them over."

"There is much bitterness to undo."

"Korr will help you."

"I am beginning to believe he is naught but a myth, made up to give hope to a badly oppressed people."

Before Sheela could reply, an ill-clad youth sidled up to them. "You are the ones seeking Korr?" he whispered.

"We are," Sumara confirmed.

He cast a furtive glance about, and, satisfied that no one was concerned with them, turned back to the women. "I will take you to him . . . for a price." He grinned, showing small crooked teeth, and held out a grimy palm.

Sumara firmly folded her arms and fastened her large blue eyes on his. "You will be paid *when* I meet Korr."

The ratlike youth mulled over her words, reluctance plain upon his face. But Sumara's icy demeanor made plain that she would brook no haggling. He nodded, his crooked grin returning, and beckoned to them. "Come with me."

The women exchanged wary glances as they slowly stood and trailed after the grinning youth. Though Tokar had said that Korr would contact Sumara, Sheela had an unsettling feeling that all was not quite right. And when they crossed the square and entered a gaping dark arch, then found themselves traversing a twisting maze of shadowy alleys, she felt certain that something was amiss. Sumara shared her misgiving, for she half-drew her sword and asked:

"How much farther?"

The youth's crooked teeth glinted in the dimness like those of a small animal's, and his reply was much too glib for comfort. "He awaits us around this next corner." He hurried ahead of them, keeping out of arm's reach. The women lengthened their strides, but he disappeared around the dark corner. Sumara quietly drew her sword, and, with tense expectancy, they rounded the corner.

They emerged into a wide garbage and rubble-strewn area, with several yawning alleyways also emptying into it. The shuffle of sandaled feet drew their attention to a nearby mound of rubble. A dozen ragtag men, knives, swords and clubs in hand, crept forward like a starving wolf pack. A bullish, black curly-bearded man with a whip-scarred face stepped from the group and tossed a coin to the youth, who leaped into the air to catch it.

"There's your reward, boy. Now begone!"

The youth gnawed the coin, then, satisfied it was real, grinned and, without a backward glance at the betrayed women, scampered off, toward another alley. The scuff of bare feet on broken pavement drew Sheela's eyes from the ratlike youth, to the alley they had just quitted. Shadows detached themselves from its sides and slunk forward, becoming the shapes of armed men. Betraying no hint of fear, Sumara maintained a commanding presence and kept her eyes on the motley group before them.

"We seek Korr."

The bullish man tugged at his curly black beard as he sharply studied the women. "So we have heard." He grinned harshly, revealing a mouthful of broken, rotting teeth. "And we have ways of dealing with the king's spies."

"We are no spies for the king," Sumara stated firmly.

"No?" scoffed the black-bearded man. He ran his gimlet eyes over them and pointed to their feet. "Then, judging by your boots, you are members of Sumara's band of Amazon bitches!"

Sumara appeared surprised. "We bought these boots from a caravan merchant with whom we traveled."

"We are from the Northern Forest Lands," Sheela added.

"Those will be the last lies you tell. When we are done, your bodies will be displayed outside of town—to serve as warning to Sumara and her outlaws!"

As the grim band edged forward, slowly widening to entrap them, Sumara desperately sought to forestall the rush. "You speak of outlaws, yet you appear no more than cowardly thieves, luring strangers into dark alleyways, to rob and murder them!" The line wavered, awaiting the black beard's response. Sumara used that delay to draw Sheela behind her with one black gloved hand.

"Aye, we be the town thieves and cutpurses," spoke their leader, "but we also be its protectors and executioners. And all my instincts tell me you are not innocent strangers." A crafty smile lit his face. "Now throw down your sword and I promise you a speedy and painless death."

Their movements so slight as to appear unnoticed, the women had wisely used the delay to put more distance between them and their antagonists and they were now near a pile of rubble. Sheela was thankful that the small band blocking the alley seemed content to serve that purpose and had not budged from their position. Sumara's smile was both deadly and alluring, and her purring voice almost seductive, as she addressed the black-bearded leader:

"And I promise you a most excruciating end, if you do not depart from us this instant."

Their howls echoing through the square, the men rushed the two women. As expected, black beard was not in the forefront but remained behind, waving his sword and urging his men on, like a general commanding an army.

As the rush came, Sumara whipped off her torn cape and flung it into the faces of the nearest men. Then, wielding her blade in a flashing arc, so quickly that Sheela's eyes could scarce follow its blur, she laid into the men who closed on one side of her. Steel rang sharply upon steel as Sumara's long blade struck sudden death among the surprised men, whose snarls abruptly became yelps of pain. A man fell, his head opened from crown to chin. Another reeled away spilling out a crimson trail of tangled entrails. Hindered by their closeness, the men fought thin air and inflicted wounds upon one another as Sumara's lithe form kept up a stream of steady motion: weaving, dodging, darting forward and back, her flickering sword forging a ring of steel about herself and Sheela.

"I am unarmed!" Sheela called in reminder, as she picked up a hunk of mud and stone from the rubble in both hands and hurled it into the face of an attacker with a raised spiked club. Nose flattened, his face crushed into red ruin, the man went down like a poled ox.

"You will soon have a sword," Sumara cried, gracefully writhing away from several thrusting swords and severing an unprotected thigh to the bone. Shrieking, the man fell backward and lay clutching his leg, in a vain attempt to stave the spurting blood. A man overreached with a wild lunge and withdrew a bloodied stump, instead of an arm. Sumara kicked the inhuman object that lay at her feet back toward Sheela. "There is your sword!" she called and sprung back into the fray.

Sheela stared down at the twitching arm, spouting red from its separated end, and the sword clutched in its lifeless hand. The thought of what must be done was repugnant—but this was neither the time nor place for squeamishness. Choking back the bile that rose in her throat, she bent and, shuddering as she worked, hastily pried the nerveless fingers from their tight grip about the hilt. Then she rose, sword in hand, and joined Sumara. She was not a moment too soon, for black beard had summoned the band from the alley as reinforcements.

Back to back they stood, as the bunch swirled about them. A man flung himself at Sheela, only to go down beneath her striking blade, split crosswise from shoulder to thigh.

"So you *can* fight," laughed Sumara, beating back a blade that was meant to stove in her raven head.

"When I must," Sheela replied, instinctively parrying a sword without being aware that she had seen the thrust, then sliding her blade beneath it and piercing her attacker's bony bare chest.

Corpses cluttered the ground, their gore making footing unsteady, as the women continued to take a bloody toll. Suddenly the youth burst from an alley, gave a shrill whistle, then called to black beard:

"Soldiers are coming!"

It was with no reluctance that the survivors gave back from the women and made a mad break for the nearest alley. Having given his news, the youth lingered for but a moment, to gape with bulging, fear-stricken eyes at the two women standing amid the scattered corpses. With a terrified cry, he whirled and fled back into the alley, as though all the fiends of Hades were fast upon his heels. No sooner had he been swallowed by its dark recesses, than the pounding of heavy boots and the rattle of swords echoed from a nearby alley.

The black-bearded man paused in another alleyway and turned back to the women. "We'll leave the soldiers to deal with you!"

Cupping his hands to his mouth, he bellowed, "Soldiers, hurry. We have cornered two of Sumara's Amazons!" He gave the women a mocking salute and retreated into the alley as the soldiers emerged from another across the open square.

Sword drawn, an officer rushed out, closely followed by nine soldiers with spears. Spotting the two women, they lowered their weapons and approached in a solemn line.

"Surrender!" the officer shouted.

Sheela glanced uncertainly to Sumara, who replied without hesitation, "I think not!"

"Then we will spill your blood!"

Sumara made a broad sweeping gesture with her sword and smiled her deadly smile. "You are most welcome to try."

As if seeking to aid her, the full moon chose that instant to flood the square with its light, clearly illuminating the tangled mass of butchered bodies about them. The appalling sight stunned and demoralized the soldiers and momentarily halted their advance. The officer whacked the nearest man wickedly across the shoulders with the flat of his sword.

"The advantage is ours—in both numbers and weapons!" he growled. "You can stand back and skewer the wenches without coming within their sword range!"

Heartened by his assurance of the women's vulnerability, the line moved forward once more. But their advance was most cautious.

Standing side by side, their crimson-stained swords ready, the tall, pale-haired Thorgon girl and her raven-haired counterpart stoically watched the soldiers cross the square, their evilly glimmering spearheads preceding them by five paces. Before they had faced a cowardly, ill-trained pack of scavengers; now they were pitted against professional, well-trained soldiers. Flight was impossible. There was naught to do but trust in the fates and fight bravely and well . . .

Chapter Nine

The sharp spear tips came closer.

Sheela tensed, poised to hack and batter them aside and spring past, in an attempt to reach the men beyond. The chance was slight, but the desire for life was strong.

The spear points were almost to her.

Suddenly the alley behind the men rang with the clatter of echoing hoofbeats. The soldiers' advance halted; heads turned back to the alley. Out charged a black clad horseman. Brawny and towering, he appeared even more titanic astride his massive black steed. A long straight sword gleamed in one raised hand. Straight toward the startled soldiers he rode.

A second horseman raced from the alley.

Though not so tall or broad as his companion, he and his sword appeared equally formidable. Whooping lustily, he galloped after the tall man.

The women were forgotten as the soldiers gave full attention to the menacing intruders. Despite their officer's shouts, they instinctively drew together like sheep, and thus unwittingly ensured their own destruction. The horsemen rode through their ranks, leaving a red wake of hacked and trampled bodies. The officer made a brave and foolhardy attempt to slash the tall man from his saddle as he swept past.

Rising in his stirrups, the brawny man put his weight behind a downward swing and cleft the officer's helmeted skull to its chin as easily as if it were a dry gourd. Then he reined in his mount beside Sumara and extended a bare sinewy arm to her.

"Quickly, Princess!" his voice boomed urgently.

Sumara took his arm without question and was lifted from the ground as though she were a child and placed behind him. His comrade helped Sheela astride his horse, then they rode back toward the soldiers. Daunted by the havoc spread by the horsemen's first charge, the soldiers fell away, clearing a wide path for them. Several spears were wildly hurled after the departing riders, but the throwers' haste caused all to broadly miss their targets. Then naught but vengeful curses followed the riders as they galloped into a darkened alley, which reverberated with their horses' fading hoofbeats.

As they rode out onto the main street, they encountered a squad of soldiers hurrying toward the alley. Wheeling their mounts, they galloped pell-mell down the winding street with the soldiers pounding after them. The soldiers' cries alerted a group of other soldiers in front of a tavern, who hastily mounted and raced after the fugitives.

As the men and women approached the main gate, two guards called for them to halt and moved to block the way. It was an empty gesture. On seeing the horsemen's intent, they dove to either side of the gate, and narrowly managed to save life and limb. The riders galloped through the open gate and out into the night. The guards clambered to their feet and watched the mounted soldiers race past, then once more took their positions on either side of the gate.

The women's extra weight did little to slow the men's sturdy mounts, and the pursuing soldiers were outdistanced as the chase led across a small plain and into a group of foothills. Losing the soldiers in the foothills, the men headed their horses up a twisting mountain trail that was little more than a goat path. Their pace slowed, as the men allowed the horses to pick their way. The brilliant moonlight revealed a sheer drop to a jagged rock floor, far below, and the women clung to the men and kept their eyes averted from the dizzying and unsettling sight. The tortuous trail continued to climb, then leveled off and broadened into a small valley. Soon they came to a wooded area and found themselves in a clearing, bisected by a stream, with a waterfall beyond.

"We will be safe here," declared the muscular man, reining in his mount and making a sweeping gesture. "This grove is considered sacred."

The four dismounted, and the men and women stood appraising one another. Without his horse, the tall man was still a commanding figure. His black leather jerkin and matching tight breeches, tucked into soft leather boots, emphasized his broad chest and shoulders and mighty-thewed limbs. Beneath a crown of thick, unruly black hair, his rugged yet not unhandsome features bespoke both strength and intelligence. The mirth that shone in his dark eyes indicated that here was a man who did not take life or himself too seriously, and who was capable of compassion. His companion was grizzled, in his middle years, and had a soldier's bearing.

"You arrived at a most fortuitous moment," Sumara said, awkwardly breaking the silence.

The tall man grinned, showing strong white teeth. "On awakening this morning, I had a vision. An old man clad in black appeared before me and said that you were ready to open your heart to your people, Princess Sumara. He then told me where I might find you and Queen Sheela of the Thorgons."

Sumara was completely taken aback by his tale. Repressing a smile, Sheela immediately thought of old Tokar, and what a busy morning he must have had. Sumara shook her head in confusion, then her large blue eyes quickened with interest.

"Why should you concern yourself?"

"Because you came to the town seeking me. I am Korr." He smiled at her unconcealed surprise and motioned to the grizzled man. "And this is my companion Zohak. We have been together since we were campaigners with Balajar the conqueror."

"Aye," Zohak agreed. "We have seen most of the known world, and learned the wisdom of each country."

Sumara directed her eyes back to Korr and smiled self-consciously. "I had imagined you a meek, priestly man. Instead I find a soldier."

"Having watched Balajar's mighty empire crumble within a year of his death, I have given up all dreams of glory and returned to aid my people."

"They speak of you in the most glowing of terms."

"That is true. But I am no holy man. Besides teaching them to better their lives, I am training an underground army to over-throw the king—when the *right* leader has appeared."

Sumara's eyes narrowed in suspicion. "And who might that be?"

"I have never lost hope that you would change and be a friend of your people," he said earnestly.

"And were I to do so, you would have your army serve me?"

Korr answered without hesitation. "At such time that you have proved your sin-cerity by your deeds." Noting her stern features, he added, "By then you will also have won the people to your cause." Though she made no reply, Sumara's face softened and became thoughtful. Korr untied a blan-ket from behind his saddle and spread it beneath a tree, beside the blanket Zohak had already spread. "Now you and Queen Sheela must rest. We will talk further in the morning. There is little time, and I have much to impart to you."

"I will be most anxious to listen."

Needing no second bidding, Sheela stretched out beside Sumara on the blankets, and was asleep within seconds.

The early morning sunlight filtering through the branches above woke Sheela from her sound sleep. She threw back the blanket, sat up, and stretched. For the first night since she had entered this Southern land, she had slept without fear, and, as a result, she was refreshed and cheerful. She glanced over, saw that Sumara's blanket was empty, and looked about for her.

"Good morrow, Queen Sheela," called a friendly voice.

Sheela turned and saw Zohak across the clearing, roasting several strips of meat over a small campfire. She smiled and stood. "Good morrow, Zohak. Where are the others?"

"They have left to talk and meditate in private." He shrugged. "I feel they will be gone most of this day. I am to do my humble best to help pass the time, by regaling you with tales of the wonders I have seen during my travels."

Sheela moved to join him. "You will find me most attentive. I desire to learn all I can about the knowledge of other countries."

Zohak grinned up at her from across the campfire. "There is nothing I like better than an appreciative listener." He motioned down at the meat cooking on sticks. "Breakfast is not yet done. Should you wish to avail yourself of yonder stream, please feel free. I will not look."

Sheela did not have to ponder his suggestion. "Thank you, Zohak. I shall do just that."

Zohak nodded. "I will call you when the meat is done."

Modesty bade Sheela to undress behind a clump of bushes before plunging into the icy stream. After the initial shock, the water was most soothing and invigorating. As she luxuriated, she thought of the cold fresh streams of her homeland, and of happier times. Before she could surrender to the melancholy which subtly began to press upon those memories, Zohak's voice called her to breakfast.

Sheela spent most of the day spellbound by Zohak's tales. She learned of magnificent cities and the courts and customs of their rulers; sacred temples hidden away on towering, snow-clad mountaintops, or in strange forests called jungles, filled with exotic animals and plant-life.

As the sun was giving way to twilight, Korr and Sumara returned. Though she maintained her proud bearing, her haughtiness was gone, and her face had a softer, more radiant glow. Zohak withdrew, and Sumara sat beside Sheela and spoke with quiet sincerity.

"I now realize that I have been mistaken in my actions, and I have many amends to make. My first is to apologize to you, Queen Sheela, and beg your forgiveness for my previous harsh treatment."

Sheela was speechless; this was most certainly a different Sumara, and a far more likable one, at that. She took her hand in both of hers. "I do accept your most kind apology, and bear you no ill will."

"Then we are friends?" the princess asked hesitantly.

Sheela smiled and squeezed her hand most reassuringly. "We are friends." Sumara beamed and placed her other hand on top of Sheela's. As incredible as it had seemed earlier, old Tokar had been right; she and her former adversary now truly shared the warmth of friendship.

* * *

They left the clearing and rode down another mountain trail to a small village, where Korr and Zohak procured horses for the women.

"We must now take our leave of you," Korr said.

"When shall we meet again?" Sumara asked, trying to hide her disappointment.

"As soon as the army is battle-ready, and you have proved your good intentions."

Sumara smiled radiantly. "That will be *soon*."

Korr returned her smile. "That is my sincere hope, Your Highness." Then he and Zohak turned their horses and rode away. As they stared after the departing horsemen, Sheela curiously noted Sumara's expression—it was that of a woman in love.

It was a two day ride to Sumara's camp, and during most of that time Sumara filled Sheela's ears with talk of Korr; her praise was as lavish as any of the townspeople they had spoken with. Though Sheela was beginning to tire of his name, she was most thankful to Korr for the wondrous change he had wrought in Sumara. She was a pleasant traveling companion, and Sheela found herself truly enjoying their friendship.

216

As they rode into the narrow pass to Sumara's camp, the four guards eagerly cheered Sumara's safe return. And, upon their entrance to the camp, they were beseiged by a cheering throng of women warriors through their journey to Sumara's tent. Sheela reflected upon this marked difference from her first arrival, at the end of Zambra's rope. Hardly had she dismissed the memory from her mind, than Zambra appeared from inside Sumara's tent. She greeted Sumara warmly, then fixed her almond eyes harshly upon Sheela.

"Princess, why have you allowed this slave to ride beside you like an equal?"

Sumara dismounted and eyed Zambra firmly. "Queen Sheela is my valued friend and ally—and is to be treated accordingly." The tall Amazon reacted with utter surprise. She opened her mouth to give protest, but the princess spoke first, closing the matter. "That is my royal command, to one and all." Her face flushing in anger, Zambra managed a stiff nod of obedience. "I will hold council within the hour," Sumara said, "and all are to attend." Again Zambra nodded stiffly. Her eyes watched most murderously as the Thorgon girl dismounted and entered the tent with Sumara.

After they had washed away the dust of

their journey, Sumara attired herself in the resplendent gold costume she had worn when she and Sheela first met. And, at her insistence, Sheela was dressed in silver breastplates, a dazzling, jewel encrusted silver girdle, and long-thonged, high-heeled silver sandals; a silver armlet, bracelets and ornate jeweled necklace completed her attire.

"I cannot accept such finery," Sheela protested, staring in wonder at her mirrored image.

"Nonsense," Sumara replied, smiling. "To command respect, a queen must dress the part." Before the young queen could further protest, she added, "Consider those as gifts to seal our friendship."

"But I have naught to offer in return."

"You have done far more for me. Because of your wisdom, I shall soon regain my throne." Though Sheela's barbarian sense of honor felt a pang of guilt at not including Tokar and the demon Lanzad in Sumara's praise, she kept silent. It was most refreshing to be praised for her wisdom, instead of being thought a "stupid, North Land barbarian." "There will be more gifts later," Sumara said. "But now, we must join the others in council." She turned and led the way through the curtained rooms of the large tent, to her audience room.

With Sheela standing behind and to one side of her, Sumara paced about before Zambra and seven women. "I have called this council to state my new policies," she announced. "Henceforth, all slaves, both men and women, are free persons and shall be treated as equals." She paused, looking about at the stunned faces before continuing. "Our raids will be confined to the king's soldiers. Money taken from the tax collectors will be returned to the people—and half the money taken from the king's tariff collectors will be returned to the caravans." The women exchanged unhappy glances; then Zambra stepped forward, to put their grievances to Sumara.

"But, Princess Sumara, surely—"

"I am not done, Zambra," interrupted Sumara. The woman nodded obediently and stepped back, directing her angry gaze at Sheela. Sumara eyed the group solemnly. "I have made an alliance with Velor the bandit. He is now a general in my army. He and his men will be arriving before this week is done."

While the other women began to murmur among themselves, Zambra disregarded their chatter and stepped forward. "You are forsaking all that we have been fighting for!"

Sumara's blue eyes flashed, but she maintained her self-control. "I am not forsaking my desire to be queen—and that alone is what you are fighting for!"

Zambra fumed. "Since your return I do not recognize the ruler I intended to serve." She pointed toward Sheela and advanced. "This pale-haired barbarian has bewitched you. She has been elevated from slave to queen, as her fine garments confirm. And now you do as *she* bids!" She halted before the Thorgon girl and glowered down at her venomously.

Sheela met her gaze evenly and replied with a quiet firmness, "That is a lie." The words had no more left her mouth, than Zambra almost knocked her to the ground with a sharp backhanded blow. Though half dazed, Sheela disregarded her smarting cheek and returned the blow with an equal force, shaking Zambra right down to her boots. Snarling an angry oath, the Amazon grasped her sword hilt.

"Hold!" shouted the inflamed princess, rushing to them.

Zambra paused, her sword half drawn, and, her eyes not leaving Sheela, spoke in a quiet, deadly tone. "The challenge has been given and accepted. Even a ruler is unable to interfere in a matter of honor."

Sumara strove to contain her anger. "No matter the outcome, my decision stands. Now withdraw the—"

"No!"

Seething with impotent rage, Sumara turned from Zambra to Sheela. "You need not accept." Her eyes pleaded with her.

Though touched by Sumara's genuine concern, Sheela shook her head. "It will only fester, otherwise."

Sumara reluctantly nodded. She was thoughtful for a moment, then directed her sharp gaze to Zambra. "True, I cannot intervene . . . but I am within my right to demand a pledge from both of you that honors will be satisfied at the drawing of first blood."

The Amazon could scarce conceal her outrage. "You seek to protect—"

"I seek to protect the both of you!" Sumara snapped. "I need able warriors—not cripples or corpses. Now if you insist upon this vainglorious show, I'll first have your word."

Scowling darkly, Zambra nodded and muttered, "As you will . . ."

Sumara looked to Sheela who nodded and said, " 'I give my royal word." Though she had been satisfied, Sumara's beautiful face was still troubled. Inwardly Sheela was even more troubled—it was she who had to fight Zambra.

The entire camp of both warriors and newly-freed male and female slaves had gathered in the wide area which separated Sumara's huge tent from the rest of the village. It was far too soon for old habits to change, and segregation still ruled, with the warriors claiming the shady side leaving the former slaves to face the sun. Still, there was a festive air, and wagering was heavy. Zambra was widely favored, particularly with the warriors, while Sheela was the former slaves' champion. Aware that the duel was to be only first blood, there were many who secretly hoped that the wound would be fatal—especially to Zambra.

Having changed into her boots and leathers, Sheela entered the wide circle formed by the boisterous crowd. As she moved to join Zambra, already waiting in the center, she caught sight of a tall, lean figure, grinning at her from beside Sumara's canopied chair.

It was Alon.

Sheela paused in mid-step and smiled warmly. Not only had Sumara kept her word to find Alon, she had taken care that she would see him before the duel. It would have been most distracting, perhaps even fatal, to have caught sight of him during the contest. Like a true friend, Sumara was doing all within her power to ensure her safe victory. As she had bestowed another gift upon her, a long, sharp, finely-balanced sword, Sumara had warned that Zambra was full of deadly tricks and foul deceptions, and should not be dealt with as one would an honest fighter.

"I see Your Highness has put away her finery, so as not to stain it with *royal* blood," taunted Zambra, as Sheela stopped several paces from her.

Sheela smiled mirthlessly. "Rather, I did not want it tainted with braggart's blood, which is most offensive and extremely difficult to remove."

"We shall see how witty you are when I have done with you, *Your Highness*," the Amazon said, her eyes ablaze.

Then Sumara's voice interrupted their repartee, and the crowd fell silent. "Once more I remind you of your pledges that first blood settles this matter of honor." Both women nodded in agreement. "Very well . . . begin!"

The women closed warily, their blades engaging in quick, tentative cuts and thrusts, each probing the other's defense. Despite their mutual dislike, both held much esteem for the other's fighting ability and neither was game to take chances. Again and again steel rang upon steel, followed by the grating of metal sliding off metal, as the two circled, exchanging cautious slashes, feints and parries. Then, with a savage cry, Zambra launched a lightning attack, her blade a silvery flaming arc in the bright sunlight. Dodging, side-stepping, parrying with expert skill, the Thorgon girl fended off the whirlwind attack. Her rival was swift and deadly, and Sheela was hard-pressed to protect herself.

As the fierce attack continued, Sheela realized that Zambra sought to beat down her guard by sheer strength and quickly end the contest. Determined that should not happen she skillfully turned aside her strokes before their full impact could be realized. Still, it was a question of whose arm would first weaken.

Seeing that her strokes were for naught, Zambra withdrew and resumed a series of cautious strokes and thrusts. The attack had reaffirmed to Sheela that her foe was no mean swordswoman, and she knew she must exercise great care. The crowd became restless, impatient for blood, but Sheela closed her ears and held her concentration.

Zambra came in screaming. She feinted a cut at Sheela's head, then quickly arced her blade downward and slashed at her ankle. Leaping back nimbly, Sheela parried the hamstring cut. Then, wielding her blade with all her strength and craft, she beat back the taller woman's persistent attack.

Their blades locked, and they stood face to face, straining. Zambra's snarling face pushed closer. Sheela felt her hot breath upon her as it whistled through the Amazon's bared teeth.

Suddenly the wench spat full into her face.

Startled and momentarily blinded by spittle, Sheela was off-guard. Before she could recover, she felt Zambra's fist drive hard into her firm, flat belly. As she swayed, striving not to cave in with pain, Sumara's warnings rang in her ears—too late. Then a terrific shove sent her reeling backward and sprawling to the ground, in a most ungainly fashion. Somehow, she managed to retain her sword.

Pain and spittle blurred her vision, and the howling crowd nigh deafened her ears to the danger of her enemy's approaching footfalls. As Zambra's shadow loomed over her, she instantly threw herself aside. She felt a rush of air and heard a sword stab into the ground, narrowly missing her rolling form. Hastily wiping her eyes, she sat up and saw Zambra bending over her, sword shoved deeply into the ground in the spot where she had lain. Before the woman could free her blade, the Thorgon girl made a reaching slash. Her sword tip grazed Zambra's upper arm, bringing blood. More surprised than hurt, the Amazon recoiled, leaving her sword swaying in the earth. Her face darkened with rage as she stared at the blood seeping between her clutching fingers. Sheela gained her feet and calmly met her adversary's blighting gaze.

The crowd was silent, most amazed by Sheela's victory. Then Sumara's firm voice called, "It is done!" A clamor erupted from the crowd, all talking at once.

Sheela turned from Zambra and strode toward Sumara and Alon, who started forward to meet her. He abruptly stopped, consternation upon his face, and shouted something that was lost in the noisome crowd. Behind him, Sumara's face went ashen. Then the pale-haired girl saw Zambra's shadow, sword raised, merging with her own. Swiftly she dropped into a crouch and whirled as Zambra's blade swooshed above her, exactly where her head had been. She made a desperate jab, but the flame-haired woman twisted aside and the blade missed by a hairbreadth. She danced sideward, and

Sheela used the opportunity to rise and turn to face her.

The crowd was mute; even Zambra's following were stunned by her unchivalrous deed. "Zambra, cease!" cried Sumara's furious voice. But the Amazon paid her no heed and launched a frenzied attack.

The affront to Sheela's barbarian sense of honesty and fairness sent her into a berserk rage. Blue sparks leaped from their blades as she met Zambra's attack with a thirst for raw vengeance.

The fury left Zambra's face as she was forced to retreat steadily. She cut madly at Sheela, only to have her blade easily parried. She had cast all upon a desperate attack, and failed. Though she continued to hold a good defense with her flailing sword, her pale-haired opponent's savage swiftness of eye and hand and foot threatened to overcome her.

Thrusting, slashing and parrying, Sheela relentlessly bore toward Zambra, who was hard put to maintain her guard. As she continued to rain mighty blows, she saw the woman's strength begin to fail, no match for the rage that she had incited. Ruthlessly Sheela attacked, beat down Zambra's weakening guard, then, with a powerful two-handed blow, knocked the sword from her hand and sent it spiraling high into the air, to land a good distance away.

The crowd screamed its delight, then abruptly fell silent, watching and waiting.

Trembling with rage, Sheela placed her sword tip between Zambra's large firm breasts and glared into her face. The truculent amber eyes met hers evenly, showing no fear and asking no quarter. Sheela was unimpressed; that was the way one should die. She was poised to thrust, when her barbarian's sense of honor suddenly stayed her hand. She would be breaking her vow to Sumara by taking Zambra's life, however pleasurable the act would be. With enormous difficulty, she quelled her rage. Yet her voice quavered when she spoke.

"I'll not break my vow. You may keep your wretched life, bitch!"

Zambra met her eyes stoically. Sheela still seethed. She would not allow Zambra or the onlookers to believe that she had been dissuaded by her display of fatalism. With a flick of her wrist, Sheela slashed the strip of fur from her foe's breasts. Then a quick stroke cut the knot holding her loincloth, and Zambra stood naked before all. She flushed in humiliation as a howl of derisive laughter went up from the spectators. Smiling, Sheela turned and strode away, leaving the Amazon modestly covering herself with her arms as the men laughed uproariously and shouted rude remarks.

Alon rushed to Sheela, exuberantly lifted her off the ground and swung her around as he congratulated her. Then he lowered her and kissed her impulsively. Letting the sword fall from her hand, Sheela placed her arms about his neck and returned his kiss. For a long moment they stood, oblivious to all else but the touch of their lips and the feel of each other's body. Then reason returned, and they parted, both lowering their eyes and smiling awkwardly. Before either could speak, Sumara, her face a mask of rage, swept past, followed by several warriors, and strode toward Zambra. Alon and Sheela turned curious eyes after her.

Zambra took a cape hastily provided by one of her warriors and covered her nakedness as Sumara stalked up to her. Unscathed by her wrathful gaze, the Amazon stared back at her sullenly, which only served to further provoke the princess' ire.

"Take those who will follow you and leave this camp with haste," Sumara commanded icily.

"Gladly!" Zambra cried. "You are no longer one that I wish to serve." She whirled and stalked away.

Sumara turned and addressed the stilled crowd. "You have been made aware of my new policies. Any who disagree may accompany Zambra when she departs!"

A long silence reigned. Then a small group of warriors detached themselves from the crowd and moved to join Zambra and her band. Sumara waited, secretly thankful when no more followed them.

Within the hour Sumara, with Sheela and Alon by her side, stood watching Zambra and her band ride from the camp. "Better to be rid of all dissidents now, than face trouble later," the princess said.

"Let us hope this is the last we will ever see of Zambra," Sheela said.

"One of you should put an end to her now," Alon said dispassionately, "otherwise, it will have to be done later." The women turned to him questioningly. "You have both made a wicked enemy, and she'll not forget."

"Zambra and I have been friends until this day," Sumara said with a trace of sadness. "I cannot believe that she will come against me."

"Let us hope that you do not rue your charity, Princess," Alon said, his eyes leveled on the Amazon and her band.

The Nomad Queen

As they watched the last riders file into the narrow pass, Sheela hoped that Alon's pessimism was misplaced; she certainly had no desire for another encounter with Zambra.

Chapter Ten

On the royal archery range behind the palace, King Jator was engaged in his favorite pastime, which he only enjoyed when using live targets. Prisoners were fair game, but when there was an insufficient supply, the young king insisted upon using his own pages. At the moment, the last of six criminals screamed and writhed with an arrow in his intestines on the target to which he was spread-eagled, and ignored the royal command to keep silent.

Heedless of the man's suffering, Jator turned cold gray eyes upon his six well-fed, magnificently-attired generals and smiled mirthlessly, his skeletal features taking on the frightening resemblance of a death skull.

"I hope that I have properly impressed you gentlemen with my archery skills," Jator said, "for it is now time for serious discussion."

The middle-aged men cast their eyes along the row of targets, each bearing a bloody victim, and at the bows and quivers hanging from posts set at intervals before the targets. It was a most unnerving sight, especially to men who had obtained their commissions through court politics, and not courage or the ability to command. There was much sheepish shuffling of feet and clearing of throats, for all knew well the subject to be discussed; and the wretch's screams did naught to help compose one's thoughts.

"For well over a month my outlaw sister, Sumara, has solely harassed my soldiers and tax collectors," Jator said gravely. "And now the people are beginning to sing her praise." He took an arrow from the quiver on the post before him and casually nocked his bow. "Need I stress upon you, my generals, that it is not pleasing to me!"

The bowstring twanged and the screeching shaft pierced the man's heart, ending his misery—and his most annoying screams.

"We are doing our best, sire," said General Retik, who, as senior officer, was the reluctant spokesman for the group.

Drawing his tall, gaunt frame erect, Jator glowered down at the shorter, pot-bellied man. "Then I would hate to see you at your worst."

Perspiration beaded Retik's broad forehead, despite the coolness of the day. "It is most difficult, now that she has allied herself with the bandit Velor."

Araxi, a gray-bearded man, tall and thick of body, nodded. "Aye, Your Highness, their combined forces outnumber most of our garrisons. If we send out a small patrol, it does not come back."

"And a large patrol rarely sights the brigands," Retik said, somewhat bolstered by Araxi coming to his defense.

Jator's gray eyes sharpened and his voice was heavy with sarcasm. "So you are content to cower behind your walls and leave the countryside to the bandits—well, I am not!" He allowed the men to sweat and fidget a moment before he continued. "Unless Sumara is stopped immediately the people will flock to her cause." He paused, to stress the importance of what was to come. "And then there will be a mass uprising that we will be hard put to suppress."

The men exchanged uneasy glances. Then Araxi spoke. "We must have more men for such an undertaking."

Jator shrugged indifferently and took another arrow from the quiver. "Then turn out the press gangs in every town and village. And triple the reward on Sumara's head—quadruple, should she be brought to me alive." He smiled, imagining the exquisite torments, both sexual and physical, he would inflict upon her beautiful, helpless body.

"Immediately, Your Highness," Retik said, with a subservient bow.

Jator slowly nocked his bow. "I expect results. I should regret to see your careers end upon the royal archery range." He suddenly spun and unleashed his arrow—straight into the heart of an unsuspecting page standing near a door to the palace. Jator savored the youth's wide-eyed pain and surprise as his body spasmed, then fell, face forward, to the ground. Lowering his bow, Jator turned to the men and was pleased to see that they were suitably intimidated. He smiled his death's head smile and said politely, "You are dismissed."

With hasty bows, the men retreated toward the palace, leaving Jator to devise new amusements until dinner.

At times, it was *so* trying to be king.

Accompanied by Alon, Velor and Sheela, Sumara emerged from her tent and saw

Korr ride up, flanked by an escort of two women warriors. Sheela could not help but notice her friend's unconcealed joy. She was beaming like a young girl with her first love. They watched the big man rein to a halt and bound from the saddle. He bowed to her, then grinned.

"You have kept your word, Princess Sumara, and I have kept mine." He make a sweeping gesture back toward the narrow pass. "Your army is camped less than an hour's ride away."

Sumara's usually authoritative voice was most demure as she spoke. "They are most welcome in this camp."

Korr shook his head. "It is now time to march on the king's capital city."

"The people are with me?"

Korr nodded. "More than ever, since the king's press gangs have been emptying the towns and villages of able-bodied men."

Velor grinned wolfishly. "Then what are we waiting for—on to the capital!"

"For once, I agree with you," spoke Alon dryly.

The former bandit chief snorted and scowled, but Sumara spoke before he could retort. "Generals, must I again remind you that we are all allies, and old grudges are to be forsaken?" Eyes downcast, the two men shifted from one foot to another, like scolded little boys. "Now pass the word, and see to your men." They hastily withdrew and Sumara turned back to Korr. "Despite their blusterings, there is a friendship of sorts."

"I will accompany them," Sheela said, deciding that she should tactfully take her leave. "You and Korr have much to discuss." Sumara nodded and smiled most gratefully. Sheela watched them enter Sumara's tent, then turned and hurried after Alon and Velor.

With Korr and Sumara at its head, the army began its long, weary fortnight's march to the capital. Throngs of villagers flocked to the princess' banner along the way, swelling the ranks mightily. There were skirmishes with the king's soldiers, but it soon became evident that they were merely delaying actions while the main body of each garrison fell back to the capital, leaving the countryside unmanned.

It was midafternoon when Sumara's weary army camped at the edge of a wide plain, within sight of the city's formidable walls. An approaching caravan was turned back, as no aid or comfort could be allowed the inhabitants of the city. The fat caravan master was disgruntled at the loss of trade, but the hope that the hated king would soon be overthrown restored his good will.

That evening spies slipped out from the city and reported that the king had prepared for a long siege. On hearing the news Sumara called a council in her tent, and for several hours she and her advisers debated over how to draw the king's army out for a decisive battle. The meeting ended without a resolution. As the others left to check the night's defenses, Sumara asked Sheela to remain.

"Korr is right," she sighed, removing her gold cape and laying it on the table beside a map of the city. "A long siege will only bring plague and starvation to the city, and many innocents will suffer."

"King Jator may be as eager for battle as we are."

The princess shook her head. "Jator is cowardly, and always avoids a confrontation unless he is certain of winning." She sat in a chair and motioned the Thorgon girl to sit. "I did not ask you to stay and prolong this discussion. I wish to speak of womanly matters." Sheela nodded, selected a nearby chair and put her feet up on a leather footstool before her. Sumara curiously noted her silver high-heeled sandals and remarked, "Usually you wear your boots with your leathers."

"I was preparing to bathe when your messenger urgently summoned me." She smiled wryly. "And after the rigors of the day my feet mutinied at the thought of re-entering those boots." Sumara smiled and fidgeted in her chair. Sheela felt she was summoning the courage to speak of something that was most personal and important to her. Sumara timidly spoke.

"You know of my deep feelings for Korr . . ."

"I would say you are in love with him."

The princess nodded, her face radiant. Then she became gloomy. "But he appears more concerned about the people and this campaign, than he does about me. Our conversations rarely stray far from those matters."

"Have you indicated your feelings to him?"

Sumara sighed forlornly. "Ofttimes . . . And I have neither been too subtle nor too bold. Only one deaf and blind could fail to understand."

Sheela was pleased that her friend was taking her into her confidence in so delicate a matter. She pondered for a moment and thought back upon her father and brothers. "Men are more concerned with their goals, and can separate their thoughts from love. We women dwell upon love, no matter what we are doing. That is the difference between us."

Sumara frowned thoughtfully. "Though grave business was being discussed during the council, I did find my eyes and thoughts straying briefly to Korr . . ."

Sheela smiled sympathetically. "So I noticed."

Blushing self-consciously, Sumara asked in alarm, "Did any of the others?"

"It was noticeable only to another woman," Sheela reassured her. The princess drew an easy breath. "You now understand why I cannot allow myself to fall seriously in love until I have accomplished my goal and freed my homeland," the Thorgon girl said wistfully.

"But I have not accomplished mine either."

"Ah, but you soon will. It is only a matter of time."

Their conversation was interrupted by a female guard who entered and announced, "Princess Sumara, Zambra and several of her warriors are outside. She most urgently requests an audience with you."

Sumara and Sheela stared at each other in surprise. Then Sumara's face hardened.

"She probably hopes to gain fame by attaching herself to our final victory."

"You know where my feelings lie," Sheela

said, unable to conceal her disdain, "yet we may have need of her mercenaries before this is done."

Sumara considered her words, then nodded and turned to the guard. "She may enter—alone and unarmed." The guard departed, and Sumara stood and moved before her royal chair. Sheela stood but remained beside the table; she did not care to be seated in Zambra's presence, should there be any chicanery.

Visored helmet tucked under one arm and her cape thrown back to reveal she was weaponless, Zambra proudly marched into the tent. Though she saw Sheela, she did not acknowledge her presence but strode straight to Sumara, now seated in her chair, and bowed. The princess coolly studied her.

"If you have come seeking spoils after the city falls, you are sadly mistaken. There will be no looting."

"I am well aware of your new-found feelings for your people," Zambra said, her voice strangely subservient. "I ask only the privilege of serving you in your final victory."

Sumara's blue eyes narrowed with suspicion. "And that is *all* you ask?"

Suddenly there was a great commotion outside. As Sheela curiously started forward, the guard rushed inside.

"Princess, the king's troops are probing our lines with fire arrows!"

Before Sumara could respond, three of Zambra's group burst into the tent, swords drawn. One ran the guard through as she started to turn. Sheela quickly grabbed Sumara's cape from the table and hurled it at the three women. The swirling cape momentarily slowed their charge and gave Sheela time to draw her own sword. Sumara leaped up, her hand going to the dagger at her waist, but Zambra stepped forward and swung her heavy helmet. With a resounding *clang*, the helmet crashed against the side of Sumara's raven head and she collapsed back into the chair, unconscious.

Left to face the group alone, the Thorgon girl wielded her sword with a mad fury, impeding the women's advance. For a long moment the clash of swords seemed to deafen the clamor outside; then Zambra's sharp voice rang out.

"Hold, Queen Sheela—or the princess dies!"

The three women fell back, slightly lowering their blades. Sheela took a side-step, enabling her to see both Zambra and the women, and held her sword ready.

Sumara was slumped limply in her chair, her own knife pressed against her ivory throat by Zambra's hand. "Surrender or Sumara will have another mouth," she said harshly.

"She may die regardless."

"King Jator wishes her alive—if possible. Now yield and I will spare your life, as you did mine. You have my word."

"You pledged your word once before!"

"True. But that was before I owed you my life." The Amazon's face was solemn, her eyes meeting Sheela's evenly. "I live by the Warrior's Code, which dictates: *A life for a life.*"

Her well-meaning words did little to allay Sheela's mistrust. "What will then happen, should I lay down my sword?"

"You will be bound and gagged, so as not to give an alarm while we leave with the princess."

Sheela hesitated; could Zambra be trusted? One spring, a slash of her sword, and she could escape through the side of the tent. But that would be leaving Sumara to certain death before she could return with aid.

"I have no further time to waste," the Amazon leader snapped. "Do we leave here with Sumara—or her head?"

Sheela's barbarian code of honor pressed upon her thoughts. She could not allow her friend to die because of her. Alive, there was a chance of rescue. Dead, Sumara was simply and finally *dead*. Reluctantly she let the sword fall from her hand. Instantly a woman sprung forward and placed a sharp sword tip against her bare midriff. She helplessly tensed at the touch of cold steel but made no move to shy away. Her fate was in the hands of her Thorgon deities.

Sheathing their swords and withdrawing lengths of rope from beneath their capes, the other two women quickly moved to Sheela. She stood unresisting as her arms were roughly yanked behind her and tied at the wrists and arms, so tightly that her elbows touched. The sword tip never wavered, nor did the knife that Zambra held to Sumara's throat. A wadded cloth was thrust into Sheela's mouth and another strip of cloth was tied over it, securing it in place. As the two women knelt and began on the Thorgon girl's legs and ankles, the other woman sheathed her sword and strode to Zambra's side.

Stepping back from Sumara, Zambra nodded to the woman, who took ropes from under her cape and bent over her. The knife dangling from her hand, the Amazon leader smiled wickedly and strode before Sheela, who could not refrain from wincing as the women tightly knotted the thin ropes about her legs, causing her ankle and knee bones to press together so firmly that they were nigh bruised. "Now see to Sumara," she ordered. The women rose and hurried away.

Her smile widening, Zambra stepped closer and placed the knife tip beneath the Thorgon girl's chin, forcing her head back so that she had to strain to maintain her balance on her high heels. "I have thought muchly of you since our last meeting," the red-haired woman purred evilly, "and what I would do." She saw the uncertainty in her captive's large amber eyes and was most gratified. Slowly she ran the knife down the girl's slender neck. "You must keep very still," she cooed, "or I might cut you . . . badly . . ." The knife brushed the long tresses of white-golden hair back from Sheela's bare shoulder. "And you must not make me break my word."

She means to kill me! thought Sheela. Alon had warned both her and Sumara, but they had not listened. Now they would both pay the price of their kind-hearted folly. Her heart froze as the cold steel inched its way down to the crisscrossing thongs holding the narrow strip of white leather about her bold breasts.

"Though I am indebted to you," her tormentor said, her almond eyes flashing with malice, "I do not forget my humiliation at your hands." Sheela tensed expectantly, resigned to her doom.

Zambra gave a flick of the knife.

The sharp blade severed the crisscrossing thongs and the strip of leather fell, baring Sheela's firm, sculpted breasts. Another swift movement sliced the sword belt and strip of leather from about her narrow hips, leaving her smooth golden skin unmarked. Sheela's eyes widened in astonishment. She was not dead. Then Zambra savagely smote her across the face, and the impact sent her toppling to the ground. Though she managed to cushion the fall with her shoulder, her whole body was jarred and her head ached most fiercely. The Amazon's hated face was a blur, and her voice seemed distant and distorted.

"Now the debt is paid. Should we ever meet anon, I will have your life!"

"We are ready," called one of the women.

As Zambra turned, Sheela groggily lifted her head and stared past her at Sumara and the women. Her wrists and arms bound behind her, Sumara swayed unsteadily on her feet while a woman draped a cape over her shoulders, concealing her bonds. Another woman lowered the visored helmet over her gagged face, completing the disguise. "Take her outside," Zambra ordered. One woman led the way while the other two supported Sumara's unsteady form between them. Zambra turned back to Sheela and cast cold eyes down on her. "Remember my words well, *Queen* Sheela!" she hissed. Then she drew back a booted foot and kicked the helpless pale-haired girl in her stomach.

Retching for breath, Sheela jerked her knees up to her body and writhed in an anguished ball. Zambra delayed to revel in her agony, then turned on her heel and strode from the tent. Desperately fighting back nausea, which would be fatal with her mouth blocked by her tight gag, Sheela tried to breathe enough air through her nostrils, to clear her head.

She was unsuccessful.

The tent spun about her. Its bright colors dimmed to gray . . . and then black . . .

Too weak to resist, Sumara was helplessly spirited through the camp by her captors. Though the attack was waning, the fire arrows had spread their confusion well. Bands of men and women scurried about, throwing dirt and water on the multitude of small flames that dotted the camp. At a glance, their party appeared to be comrades aiding a wounded warrior to safety, and none interfered with their passage.

They slipped, unnoticed, from the camp and made their way to a spot where another woman waited with horses. Sumara was placed upon a horse, and the group rode like the wind to the city.

Two impressively-clad guardsmen threw open a set of sturdy wooden doors, and Sumara and her captors entered the king's audience room and started up the carpeted approach to the marble dais. Their spears gleaming in the light of a great candle chandelier, a long row of guardsmen stood, statuelike, on either side of the room. On the dais two guardsmen stood slightly behind the canopied throne where Jator, attired in his finest garments, languidly lounged. The fire from a nearby brazier caused the jeweled crown upon his dark head to sparkle brilliantly above his gaunt features.

The sight of this hated living skeleton caused Sumara to falter. Prodded along by the women, she moved stiff-legged, her mind conjuring up past images of the cruelties she had suffered at his hands. Icy fingers of fear played upon her spine. Her heart pounded so rapidly she thought it would deafen her ears within the encasing metal helmet. Through its narrow horizontal slits, Jator's long spi-

dery figure grew with every step she took.
Then all too quickly they were standing
before the dais, and Zambra was bowing
to the usurper-king.

"What is your news, Zambra?" Jator asked,
his cold, piercing gray eyes gleaming diaboli-
cally in the brazier's flickering light.

"The attack was timed to perfection, and
I was able to carry out my part." Zambra
stepped aside and gestured to Sumara. The
other women quickly removed the cape and
visored helmet and thrust Sumara forward.
"Here is your sister," the flame-haired Amazon announced triumphantly.

Trembling inwardly, Sumara managed,
despite her gag and bonds, a semblance
of haughtiness as she stared up at Jator,
who leaned forward eagerly on his throne
like a giant spider preparing to pounce. His
terrible, familiar death's head smile made his
face all the more loathsome.

"Welcome home, my beloved sister," he
said tonelessly. He casually beckoned with
one bony, splay-fingered hand. "You may
approach the throne and be properly recognized."

Zambra drew the scarf down from Sumara's mouth and aided her onto the first of
the steps leading up to the dais. Her legs felt
watery as she hesitantly mounted the steps,

but Sumara was determined to express only utter contempt to her despised half-brother. Yet his eyes made her feel unclean, and her flesh crawled at the thought of his touch. She wanted to spin around and bolt back down the steps and out of the room, but she knew it was hopeless. Even if her trembling legs would support her undertaking, Zambra and her warriors were waiting below, not to mention the guardsmen lining the walls. The sound of her high-heeled sandals' timid tread upon the marble steps seemed to echo through the long room—and then she stood before the throne.

"Kiss my ring in obedience," Jator said, holding out a long-fingered hand, with a large ring bearing the royal crest upon his middle finger.

"Usurper!" she spat. "You will never be my king."

Face twitching with rage, Jator withdrew his hand and glared up at her, while tightly gripping the chair's scrolled arms. It was but a moment, and he was once more relaxed, the horrible smile again upon his face. He leisurely drew his gaunt frame up from the chair and lay his hands upon Sumara's bare ivory shoulders. His gray eyes looked down at her in amusement as he felt her tense at his touch. "You need time to readjust to your former life," he said soothingly, and grinned more widely as her icy glare slipped for an instant, to reveal her underlying fear. Gently he turned her around to face the group below. "But first, dear sister, I must tend to business." He pointed down at Zambra. "You are expecting a reward for your deed?"

"I served you, and it is only just."

"Then I will be *just* with you." Though Jator smiled, his eyes were brutal and calculating. "Sumara will decide your reward." A casual wave of his hand brought the guardsmen to life.

Instantly, Zambra and the four women drew their swords. It was a needless gesture. Spears lowered, the guardsmen drew a ring of steel around the group, and there was no escape.

"What means this?" the Amazon leader shouted.

Jator answered as if to a child. "You betrayed your former mistress for the promise of gold. One day, you will deal me the same—should the price be fitting."

Zambra could make no sound reply. Slowly the blade fell from her hand; the others followed her lead. The ring of steel moved closer, forcing the women to huddle together.

Jator drew Sumara to the throne and gently pushed her down upon its seat. "I momentarily vacate my throne, which you so dearly covet, sweet sister." He removed his crown and placed it atop her raven head and bowed mockingly. Then he half-sat on one wooden arm and lightly stroked her long tresses. "Now dispense justice to this traitor." Sumara sat in silence, her eyes staring down at Zambra's grave face. Jator leaned closer, his lips brushing Sumara's ear. "May I humbly suggest several most intriguing tortures for Your Highness to consider?" Sumara remained silent. Though she wished vengeance for her betrayal, she would not indulge Jator.

Zambra and the women waited silently, showing no emotion.

Jator gave a peevish sigh. "Very well, I revoke your authority." He took the crown from Sumara's head, placed it atop his, then stood and addressed the group. "I claim these four for the royal archery range. Take them to the dungeon, where the rest of their motley group await."

"Bastard!" yelled Zambra. "May your spirit be condemned to the Dark Regions—where you will eat offal for eternity, like the vile swine that you are!" A spear butt smashed against her jaw, ending her curses, and leaving her four companions to bear her semiconscious body away.

Jator watched a group of guardsmen lead the group from the room, while the other guardsmen returned to their statuelike positions against the walls. Then he again sat on the arm of the throne, and smiled down at Sumara, who stared after the departing group. "Now I have a surprise for you," he said gleefully. "In anticipation of your return, I have ordered a feast in your honor."

An icy dagger drove straight through Sumara's heart. She turned and looked up at him, her blue eyes widening with nervous suspicion. She tensed as Jator placed a hand on her arm and ran his fingers over her tight bonds.

"And afterward, you will once more join in the festivities with my select circle of intimate friends."

Sumara recoiled against the chair as his words immediately summoned horrible memories of past indignities forced upon her. The frightening, leering skeletal face leaned closer. She felt his fingers caressing her cheek.

"You appear as fresh and unspoiled as a virgin," purred Jator. Then he winked and his smile widened. "But, of course, *we* know better."

* * *

It was well after the attackers had withdrawn, and the fires were extinguished, that Korr and Alon entered Sumara's tent, to report on the destruction, and found Sheela's trussed and gagged form thrashing, naked, upon the ground near the dead guard. Upon spying them her movements ceased, but her eyes remained wide and full of urgent messages above her gag. Springing ahead of Korr, Alon knelt beside her and tore at her gag. Then, as the men hastily freed her, Sheela told of Zambra's treachery.

Wrapped in Sumara's gold cape, Sheela sat in a chair and rubbed her rope-burned wrists, while the two men paced about discussing the grave events.

"We must keep Sumara's abduction secret," Korr said, "otherwise it will demoralize the army, and there will be a rash of desertions this night."

"But by morning King Jator will see that the news is spread," Alon said.

Korr grunted and continued pacing. Abruptly he halted and turned to Alon and Sheela. "Of course!" he cried. "This is what we have needed to draw the king's men out of the city." He noted their bewilderment and explained. "Should Jator believe that our army is breaking up, disheartened, he will order his troops to crush the rebels, once and for all."

"But Sumara must be rescued before our victory," Sheela said, "or Jator will use her to bargain with."

Korr was thoughtful for a moment. "If we can enter the city, there are members of the secret army there who will aid us."

"Exactly *how* do we enter the city?" Alon asked.

Before Korr could reply, a thought came to Sheela. "The caravan that we turned away from the city is camped not far from here." She smiled brightly. "That is how Sumara and I entered the town when we were seeking Korr."

"The caravan master is certainly no supporter of the king," Alon remarked.

Sheela pressed on enthusiastically. "And the members of the caravan will spread the tale that our army is dispersing." She looked to Korr, who had been listening in silence.

Slowly his rugged features broke into a wide grin of approval and he exclaimed, "Never underestimate the talents of a woman!"

Chapter Eleven

King Jator stood on a balcony and gazed down at the market square, separated from the palace grounds by a broad wall. He winced at the morning rays. It had been a long night of drinking and debauchery, and he was pleasantly sated. Though his head had not completely ceased its pounding, his vision was clear and his stomach remarkably settled.

The punishment block dominated the middle of the square, and it was there that Jator directed his eyes. He smiled sadistically at the sight of Sumara's tall, graceful figure tautly spread-eagled, naked, between the two posts atop the block. Guardsmen armed with crossbows lined the walls of the square, and other guardsmen, with spears, ringed the punishment block. The few people in the square went about their business and purposely kept their eyes averted from Sumara. That was most annoying to Jator. Where was the enjoyment of Sumara's humiliation, if no one stopped to gawk at her nakedness and, hopefully, not only hurl crude taunts, but offal and anything else they might lay their grubby hands upon? He turned to his two advisers and inquired:

"Why hasn't the male populace taken advantage of my most generous offer to avail themselves of a royal princess? It would seem a novelty in their drab lives."

Misak, a courtly, graying man twice the king's age, replied, "A drunkard did, Your Highness."

Jator arched an eyebrow. "I would like to have seen that."

Levon, a foppish young man not much older than Jator, smiled and shrugged. "But his pleasure was short-lived."

Misak nodded. "True. He was later found in a nearby alley, his throat cut from ear to ear."

Jator would have laughed aloud but, fearful of upsetting his hangover, settled on a smile. "Now the people are protective of her, but their loyalty will wane as the siege continues, and they are reduced to eating dogs and rats."

"That may not happen, Your Highness," Misak said. "Our scouts report that there appear to be desertions within Sumara's army."

Levon nodded and added, "And a caravan is approaching, unmolested by the rebels."

Suspicious by nature, Jator did not blindly rejoice at the encouraging news. "Tell my generals to prepare. Should this not be a ruse, my army will ride out and put an end to this annoyance—most ruthlessly!" The two men bowed and left him to continue his anxious watch for violators of Sumara's virtue.

It was midmorning when the lumbering caravan was reluctantly admitted through the city gates, and proceeded along the cobble-stoned main street toward the market square. A sullen pall hung over the city, and there was scarcely a soul on the street.

Clad in the beads, bangles and filmy silks of a dancing girl, Sheela was carried upon a litter by four burly, gay-clad slaves, while Alon, finely-dressed, and Korr, in the flowing robes of a rich merchant, rode on either side.

Sheela beckoned to Alon, who leaned sideways in his saddle, and spoke low to him. "These disguises may help us to enter the palace, but what if I am called upon to dance?"

Alon ran his eyes the length of her trim, scantily-clad figure. Then he shrugged and answered, "You, uh . . . merely shake a great deal." He grinned, but Sheela did not share his humor.

The street widened into the almost empty market square. The sight of Sumara on the punishment block, naked for all to see, shocked and incensed Sheela. A glance at her two companions showed that they shared her outrage.

"Be calm," whispered Korr. "Remember we are strangers, and have no interest in the politics of Istwar."

The caravan halted and the merchants began to unload and set up their wares. Sheela and the two men stood near the palace gates and observed Sumara and her surrounding guards. Her raven head drooping, the princess appeared oblivious to the caravan and its activities.

"How are we to rescue Sumara with guards everywhere?" Sheela asked.

Korr turned from studying the walls. "I will return later."

Sheela frowned. "Where are you going?"

"To contact our secret group within the city."

"What of us?" Alon asked.

"Remain here. When the merchants are summoned to the palace, see that you and the others secreted within the caravan accompany them."

"But Sumara is out here," Alon said.

"Aye," Korr agreed. Then he added, "But the king is inside." He half-turned, then paused and looked back at them. "No matter what is done to Sumara, short of death, you are not to act until I return. I will personally see to her rescue." He strode away, leaving Alon and Sheela to speculate on his plan.

At the end of a twisting street in the poorer section of the city, Korr stopped before a closed blacksmith's shop and beat loudly upon its doors. There was a stirring inside, then a rough voice growled:

"Closed for the day. Take your business elsewhere!"

"Open up, Thos, or I'll break these doors down around your fat ears!"

There was the sound of a bar being removed from the other side of the doors. Then one door flew inward, and a bald, goodly-sized, middle-aged man in smithy's garb stood grinning at Korr. "Then you'd best get your arse inside, you big ox!"

Korr entered, and the two men clapped each other on the back warmly. The smithy closed and replaced the bar across the doors, and called into the dim recesses of his shop, "Show yourselves, louts. This is the man we have awaited!"

A group of peasants detached themselves from the shadows and gathered in the middle of the shop. Korr had Thos kindle the fire in his furnace, while he addressed the twenty men, who were each leaders of secret groups from various parts of the city. When he had finished explaining his plan, he removed his flowing robe and stood in leather vest and breeches.

"Those of you who have blacksmith skills remain," he said. Eight of the group stepped forward. "Excellent. We have a hard task ahead, and very little time." Then, with stout iron tongs and heavy hammers, he and the men went to work constructing two long sheets of steel, thick enough to ward off arrows.

After his noon meal, King Jator returned once more to the balcony and looked down upon the market square. Though more people now wandered through the square, they appeared to discreetly ignore Sumara, who slumped limply between the two posts on the punishment block. Jator was most disappointed. Then familiar footfalls drew his attention from the square, and he turned to see Misak hastening onto the balcony. The older man bowed respectfully, then announced:

"Your Highness, a scouting party has returned, and confirms the caravan master's tale. Sumara's army is disbanding!"

"Excellent!" Jator cried, elated. "All, save the palace guards and those in the square, are to go into battle immediately." Misak bowed and started to leave, but Jator held up a hand. "After the army has left, I want preparations begun for a victory celebration." He looked down at the square. "Have the merchants bring their best wares for my inspection." He smiled as he noticed a most beauteous girl below, standing apart from the merchants, engaged in conversation with a tall, handsome man with a thin mustache. Beckoning Misak closer, he pointed down at the girl. "That tall, pale-haired dancing girl intrigues me. See that she accompanies the merchants."

Misak smiled knowingly. "Certainly, Your Highness."

Jator waved a bony hand in dismissal. "I shall be on the archery range. Inform me when the battle is done." Misak nodded and followed him inside.

Aided by Thos and several men, Korr put on the two long sheets of steel, which were attached in front and back by stout ropes across his broad shoulders. Then he was helped into his robe, which concealed his armor, and moved about, adjusting his body to the added weight.

"Your movements appear labored," Thos remarked, watching Korr's movements critically.

"That cannot be helped," Korr said. He slowly strode to one of the men and took the wine bottle from his hand. "This will explain my movements," he said, holding up the bottle. "No one expects a drunken man to walk as others do."

"That is right," Thos agreed.

Korr motioned to the men. "Now let us join the others in the square."

Sheela held her breath as she and Alon entered the king's throne room with the merchants and disguised members of Sumara's army, and saw the row of guards on either side of the room. The throne was vacant, but two guards stood on the dais.

"The king is presently occupied on the royal archery range," said the man called Lord

Misak, "but will join you soon." He then turned and went out, leaving the merchants to begin readying their wares.

As far as Sheela was concerned the king could take his time. Her summons meant there was a royal interest in her, and she would be required to dance—among other things. The ruse had been successful, and the king's army was now leaving the palace to do battle. With luck it would only be a short while until the city rose up against the king. Sheela had faith in her womanly guiles, to delay the king's amorous advances, but the thought of having to dance absolutely terrified her. She knew naught of these Southern dances, in which the woman writhed and shook to charm a man. Better to fight a dozen men in combat, than to subject her pride to ridicule by prancing about like a dancing bear. She turned to Alon and whispered:

"I hope Korr acts soon."

Alon nodded and gave her a reassuring smile. She did not feel reassured.

Through pain-dulled eyes Sumara grimly watched the last of the king's troops ride through the square past the large silent crowd that had gathered. It was evident that the army was on its way to battle. Had her capture so disheartened her army that they were disbanding? She could think of no other reason for Jator to order his army out. But then she could not think too clearly at this time.

Once more she let her head droop. It did naught to relieve the agony her tautly spread body continually felt, but it did ease her slender neck. Long ago her rigid limbs had lost most of their feeling, yet there was still an ache. The sun was past its zenith, but its cruel rays had not lessened. Her ivory skin had acquired a dark burning glow under its harsh glare. Even the stone was hot beneath her bare toes. She grimly remembered sentencing deserters and traitors, even her friend Queen Sheela, to the agonies of the sun, in the Land of the Thirsty Death—now that punishment was being enacted upon her. And Jator had promised that she would pass her days here, as long as the siege lasted. But even worse, her nights were to be spent in orgies.

Sumara vainly tried to shut out the memory of last night's sufferings from her mind. Jator had been especially vile, as were his nobles, but the slaves were the worst of the lot. Besides exulting in the opportunity to humiliate one far above their lowly station, there had been the desire to please their master, and she had been ravaged and abused most foully, to the delight of all. She shuddered at the thought of what new torments Jator's twisted mind would concoct for her tonight. Better to remain here. At least, no one had molested her since early morning, and the people in the square seemed to pay her no mind.

She became dimly aware of a commotion in the crowd. As the disturbance continued, she weakly raised her head and saw the guards, spears lowered, holding back the angry crowd as a tall man in swirling robes, a wine bottle clutched in one hand, drunkenly made his way toward her. She realized his intent and gasped and shook her head, silently imploring the gods to deliver her. But that was not to be. His movements drunken and labored, he ascended the steps, and there was naught she could do but stand helplessly waiting, her arms spread wide above her head, as though anxiously welcoming him like a beloved one.

Jeering and jostling one another, the protesting crowd pressed nearer, forcing the guards to close ranks around the punishment block. Their anger increased as the man reached the top of the steps and staggered toward her. Her stomach knotting at the thought of becoming a receptacle for his lust, she tried to shrink away as he stopped before her. The thongs about her wrists and ankles were no more unyielding than they had been with her first drunken violator.

Then she heard a familiar voice speak her name low, and looked up into the man's face. Her bleary vision cleared and she gasped in disbelief as she recognized Korr. She wanted to speak his name, but no words issued from her parched throat. Then her joy became shame, that he should witness her cruel degradation.

Waving the wine bottle, Korr said in a loud drunken voice, "Here, Princess, some wine to warm your blood before we begin!" He stepped closer and placed the bottle to her lips. "Drink and listen closely," he whispered. "When I cut you free, drop to the ground and crawl beneath my robe." Sumara nodded, partly choking on the warm wine. Korr raised the bottle to his mouth and drank deeply. As he did so, his eyes scanned the guards with crossbows on the walls above. Draining the bottle, he belched loudly, tossed it away and embraced her.

The crowd below shrieked their disapproval and surged forward while the guards desperately strove to keep them back. Korr saw the guards on the wall give their attention to the crowd and stealthily drew a knife from a sheath strapped to one forearm. He rapidly cut the long taut thongs holding Sumara's wrists, and each arm fell limply to her side with a sharp *slap*. Gripping her narrow waist to steady her, he attempted to bend and slash the thongs imprisoning her ankles, but the long steel sheet beneath his robe prevented him.

"Give me the knife!" Sumara said. Forcing her numbed fingers to respond, she took the knife and leaned over. As she sliced the thong on one ankle, a crossbow bolt screamed through the air and thudded into the post. Turning, she hastily severed the remaining thong, then dropped to the stone as Korr released her waist. Another bolt slammed into the other post, narrowly missing her raven head. Though her numbed limbs almost betrayed her, she managed to drag herself beneath the hem of Korr's robe. As she wriggled up between his body and the sheet of steel, she was almost deafened by the sound of a volley of arrows striking harmlessly against the steel. Then she and Korr were moving and more arrows were bouncing off the front and back of his armor.

The rioting crowd broke through the ring of guards surrounding the punishment block and met Korr and Sumara on the steps, engulfing them so that the guards on the walls were unable to fire a clear shot. The square became a scene of frenzied activity, as members of the underground army pulled out their concealed weapons and attacked the guards around the punishment block, and stormed the guards atop the walls.

Sumara emerged from her steel covering and was hastily given a peasant's robe to cover herself. Thos helped Korr discard his armor and thrust a sword into his hand.

"On to the palace!" Korr shouted above the noise and clatter of arms. Then, with a brawny arm protectively around Sumara, he waved his sword high and led the way toward the palace.

From street to street, house to house, news of the uprising against the hated tyrant spread. In no time, men poured into the square, replacing those who had fallen, and the mob swelled. All of one mind, they followed Korr and Sumara and stormed the palace gates.

*   *   *

From the cover of a rocky area, Velor and Zohak watched as a small band of men and women riders approached, pursued by the king's thundering host. Trampling the few remaining tents in their enthusiasm, the cavalry raced after the fleeing group and thought of the easy victory to be won. Though several seasoned subordinates strongly urged caution, General Retik and his staff paid no heed.

The chase led past the wooded area and toward the hills and rocks beyond. Then the fleeing riders abruptly spun around on their horses' backs and, bowstrings twanging in unison, sent a storm of arrows straight at their pursuers.

Screaming in pain and astonishment, the first rank went down; those not already dead when they hit the ground had the life crushed out of them by the successive ranks behind them. With vengeful yells, the cavalry continued its mad pursuit and began to gain upon their quarry.

Suddenly a sheet of arrows arched from the woods on one side of the cavalry. Men and horses went down, stirring billowing clouds of dust to add to the confusion. The running pack came to an abrupt halt and wheeled to face the oncoming horde. Then out from behind the rocks rode Velor and Zohak at the head of a huge force, which spread out into a battle line to meet the king's cavalry.

Beset by a continuous rain of arrows from the wooded area, and now facing a group of nigh equal strength, the king's once-mighty army sought to withdraw.

But a new obstacle was added.

Archers rose up from concealed pits in the ground and blocked their retreat, pouring arrows into their ranks. Scores fell. Horses reared and screamed, trampling the fallen. The ragged ranks wheeled once more, to face the mounted enemy's charge.

The waves of charging horsemen came together with a clash of steel. Velor and Zohak were in the forefront, hewing like blood-mad madmen as their group smashed through the disorganized mass. Men, women and horses went down with blood-curdling screams. The battle became a series of hundreds of single combats, with no semblance of order, save hand-to-hand butchery. The archers left their various places of concealment and joined the raging mass, dragging men from their horses and slitting their throats.

Heads flew from necks, arms from shoulders, stomachs were skewered and chests halved. Still, the dying continued unabated. Blood flowed from hundreds of sources as dead and wounded alike were trampled under foot and hoof.

A sword in either hand, Velor laughed like a fiend as he wreaked savage destruction on the foes that swirled about him. His blades cleaved flesh and bone, turning men into bloody corpses.

Surrounded by howling enemies, General Retik and his disheveled, blood-spattered staff had no choice but to fight bravely. For perhaps the first time in any of their not so illustrious careers, the palace generals wielded their swords in life or death combat. Their stand was most noble. Even when General Araxi's severed head struck his armored chest with a resounding thud and he was deluged in his friend and fellow officer's blood, General Retik did not shrink from battle. Indeed, he redoubled his efforts to break from the trap. He almost succeeded—until he ran afoul of Zohak.

Their sword-to-sword combat lasted but briefly. Blades whirled and clashed, parrying, thrusting, cutting. Then Zohak rose in his stirrups and struck solidly into the general's fat neck. The sword tore through flesh, bone and armor, and Retik's cloven body fell sideways from his horse, to be trampled into an unrecognizable mass of gory flesh.

The battle rose to a fearsome pitch, then slowly ebbed. The king's army fought and died bravely, to the last man.

Even its generals.

Sheela heard the growing clamor outside the palace and glanced anxiously to Alon. "It seems you will not have to dance after all," he remarked, with a hint of disappointment. Before she could voice her own thoughts, the doors burst open behind them and Lord Misak entered, shoving aside a merchant.

"Guards!" he shouted. "To the main doors, quickly. We are under attack!"

The orderly rows of guardsmen left their stations and hurried forward. The merchants parted to either side of the doors, allowing the guards to begin filing from the room. When half the guardsmen were out in the hall Alon nodded to his group.

Throwing off their disguises, the men attacked the guardsmen. Carpets were unrolled, spilling out swords and knives. The doors were slammed shut and the crossbar inserted, sealing off the room. While the warring factions engaged in hacking and slashing one another, the real merchants retreated to the relative safety of the far walls. At such close range the guardsmen were forced to discard their spears and rely upon their sabers.

Steel met steel with ringing force as the battle raged about the large room. Sheela nimbly avoided a sword thrust and instantly drove her sword through the guardsman's teeth; the tip of her blade met the back of his helmet with a scarping of metal. She wrenched the blade free and thrust it through his bowels for good measure.

Alon fought by her side but saw that she did not need his protection. He parried a cut at his head and his sword flashed out, skewering his opponent through the neck.

The room echoed with the horrible din of clashing blades, the chopping of steel carving flesh and bone, the curses of the living, and the shrieks of the dying. Blood, brains and entrails soiled the fine purple carpet that led to the dais and its empty throne. More accustomed to parades and guard duties, the guardsmen were no match for the determined band.

The frenetic battle was almost done, when Sheela's bare foot slipped on a thick trail of blood and down she went, to land beside a headless corpse. Her attacker rushed in and lunged down for the kill. Seizing the corpse's decapitated head from beside its body, Sheela hurled it up by its long hair.

With a sharp, meaty thud, the head struck the man in the face. He yelped and staggered, his thrust unfinished. Sheela sat up and rammed her sword upward—straight between the man's spread legs.

Screaming hideously, the man reared up on his toes, body arching, sword frozen in mid-swing. Sheela ripped her blade upward, higher, and disemboweled her foe. Alon whirled from downing a guardsman and ended the man's agony with a quick stroke that parted his head from his neck. Hastily dragging Sheela to her feet, he retreated from the gushing red shower arcing from the tottering corpse's ragged neck. The grisly thing that once was a whole man abruptly pitched forward and crashed to the floor beside the other headless body.

Alon and Sheela looked about them and saw the last three guardsmen go down, mangled and dismembered. In the startling quiet, they became aware of the sounds of a howling battle going on beyond the bolted doors. How long it had been in progress, they knew not.

"Throw open the doors!" Alon shouted. While his order was being carried out, he turned to Sheela, who was removing the last of her bloodied dancing silks and using them to wipe her blood-splotched body clean. "Are you ready to join in the fray?" he asked. She nodded, tossed aside the ruined silks, and gripped her sword. Now clad in naught but bangles, and a skimpy cloth halter and girdle, she followed Alon to the opening doors.

Chapter Twelve

The long hall resounded with sounds of battle as Alon and Sheela led their party from the throne room. Fighting with a desperate frenzy against the surging crowd, the guardsmen were slowly retreating toward them. Swords raised, Alon and Sheela charged along the hall at the head of their howling pack. Seeing that they were being fallen upon from behind, the guardsmen's disciplined retreat became a disorderly rout.

Caught in two wedges of steel, the guardsmen's ranks were split asunder and red massacre followed. Corpses piled and rivers of blood flowed through the hall. Their backs against a wall, the remaining guardsmen made a final stand. It was brief but did not lack valor. Swords flashed and clattered, men screamed and fell, bleeding and writhing in torment, adding their bodies to the fresh piles of mutilated corpses.

Then, abruptly, it was over.

Sheela spied Korr and Sumara and, with Alon, began shoving toward them through the press.

"Where is Jator?" Sumara asked anxiously as the four met.

"The royal archery range," Sheela informed her.

"This way!" the princess cried, whirling and hastily leading the three toward an adjoining hallway.

Acknowledging the polite applause led by the fawning Lord Levon, King Jator hung his bow on a post and started away from the archery range, leaving the lifeless bodies of Zambra and the last five of her band dangling from targets.

"Your Highness was most excellent today," gushed Lord Levon. Not to be outdone in bootlicking, the other six nobles hastened to add their praises.

"I am *always* excellent," Jator stated truthfully, though his extreme vanity eagerly accepted their words, however insincere.

The group trailed after him and continued trying to outdo one another with flattery. Jator abruptly halted as he caught sight of a blood-splattered figure, dripping sword in hand, racing toward him from the palace. As it drew nearer, he recognized Lord Misak.

"Your Highness," Misak shouted breathlessly, "the palace has fallen!"

Jator was rigid with shock, unable to believe his ears. A glance at his companions told that they, too, were greatly distraught. "How can this be?" he demanded of his advisers. "You assured me—"

"Sumara!" Levon interrupted, pointing toward the palace.

Jator turned and saw his half-sister, sword in hand, clad in a torn, bloodstained robe, approaching with a brawny giant in black leathers. Hurrying out of the palace after them were the pale-haired dancer and the tall man she had been talking with in the square. His face twitching with rage, Jator gestured toward the approaching group and bellowed:

"Kill them!"

The seven men drew their swords and rushed to intercept the four. Jator glared at Misak, who stood catching his breath from his exertion. "You heard my order, Misak!" The older man nodded and, with

the resignation of a condemned man, reluctantly moved away to join the others. Jator
whirled, ran to a post, snatched a bow and
full quiver of arrows, and started out onto
the range, making toward the wide area
with trees and tall grass, a short distance beyond the targets. He would be
safe there, should Sumara and her party
win their way past the nobles and come
seeking him.

Seeing her despised half-brother heading
across the archery range, Sumara veered
from the approaching nobles, in an attempt
to avoid the delay of combat. Unfortunately, she did not achieve her aim. Lord Levon
blocked her way. Another time she would
have relished killing him slowly, but now
she must dispatch him quickly.

Levon leaped forward to meet her, and
they both attacked simultaneously in a whirlwind of action. Then Sumara feinted and
lunged sideways. She felt his blade fan her
skin as it almost touched her. Her own
blade moved in a blurring arc, and there
was the sickening crunch of bone and flesh.
Slack-jawed, his eyes bulging, Levon toppled
backward, split from breastbone to groin.
Sumara spared but a glance and continued
toward the range.

The Nomad Queen

In her obsession to catch Jator, Sumara ignored the bows and quivers hanging on the various posts before the targets and ran out onto the range. As she neared a target, she saw Jator pause before the tall grass and, bow nocked, turn back to look at the battle. He spotted her and raised his bow.

As the arrow was unleashed, Sumara made a leaping dive for the cover of the target. The arrow whizzed past above, scarcely missing her raven hair. She rolled to her knees and found herself staring up into Zambra's dead face.

Her face contorted in a silent scream of anguish, Zambra stared back at her with wide, unseeing almond eyes. Arrows protruding from her limbs, stomach and chest gave testimony to the hard death she had met.

For an instant, the sight stirred compassion within Sumara. Then the remembrance of betrayal hardened her heart. She turned away and cautiously peered around the side of the target, in time to see Jator plunge into the tall grass. Gripping her sword, she leaped up and dashed after him.

While Korr and Alon, their blades clanging in unison, busied themselves with six men, Sheela was engaged with Lord Misak, who surprisingly proved himself an able fighter.

Twice she had narrowly ducked decapitating slashes. But he now was beginning to tire and sought to end the contest before his arm became leaden.

And haste was his undoing.

As Misak unbalanced himself with a wild slash, Sheela lithely ducked and, crouched low, rammed her sharp point into his guts. He fell screaming, spewing blood and entrails.

Sheela looked past the dying man and saw the princess darting across the range, toward the tall grass. She was about to go after her, but hesitated and turned to the men.

Two nobles lay gasping their last in pools of their own blood. The remaining four used caution as they pressed their attack upon Korr and Alon, whose swords wove a protective web of flashing steel. With a wicked slash Korr sent his two opponents leaping away, then spared a glance to Sheela.

"Go after Sumara!" he shouted, and turned his attention back to his prudently advancing foes.

Seeing her companions did not require her aid, the tall, pale-haired Thorgon girl made for the range. She paused to discard her sword and take a bow and quiver from a post, then started onto the range. She saw Sumara disappearing into the tall grass and called to her. Her cry went unheeded. As she stopped to slip on the quiver and nock her bow, she caught sight of Zambra's corpse hanging from a nearby target. Though the red-haired vixen had met a deserved end, Sheela regretted the lost opportunity to face her once more in combat and enact her own revenge. There was no time to waste on the dead; she ran on, hoping to catch the princess.

Sumara moved cautiously through the tall grass. Her eyes darted warily and her ears strained to hear Jator's movements. She cursed herself for not taking a bow and quiver. Her sword was of no use, unless she could get close to him—and that was something Jator would do his best to avoid.

Had she not been so intent upon Jator, she might have seen a hidden wire stretching before her feet. But it was just as well—her stumble saved her life.

With a startled gasp, Sumara pitched forward onto her knees at the instant a bow twanged. The arrow missed its mark, screaming past where she should have been standing, and struck the decaying, arrow-filled chest of a man bound to a concealed target that sprung upright from the tall grass. Recoiling from the horrid dead thing, she threw herself flat. No other arrows followed. Then she heard Jator's distant, taunting voice.

"You are now in my preserve, dear sister. Come and find me—if you dare!" His evil, slightly high-pitched laugh was heard, followed by a distant rustling of grass as he moved away.

As Sumara lay listening to his departing sounds, she grimly realized the truth of his words. This was where Jator had spent many an hour playing at hunting. She had never before ventured into this forest of horrors. She heard Sheela's voice calling to her and looked around. She was tempted to answer her, but the desire to at long last deal with Jator alone kept her silent. She cautiously rose and moved on in search of him. The odious stench of the decaying corpse lingered in her nostrils for a very long while.

Alon delivered a death-stroke, slicing his last foe open from shoulder to chest, and looked to Korr in time to see the big man dispatch his final opponent with a two-handed blow that cut through the top of the man's head, to the middle of his chest. Korr wrenched his blade free and the corpse fell, gushing a torrent of crimson, its split head dividing onto either shoulder.

"Never have I seen such a stroke," Alon said in awe.

"I only wish it had been King Jator." Korr scanned the tall grass beyond the archery range. There was no sign of the women. "Come," he said urgently, "let us find Jator before the women do."

The two men took bows and quivers from posts and raced across the open range. They paused at the edge of the tall grass and nocked their bows before entering. Eyes and ears alert, they quietly stole into the silent area.

Choking back the bile that tried to rise from her throat, Sheela stood gaping at the rotting corpse attached to a target she had just caused to spring out from behind a bush, by accidentally tripping a wire with her bare foot. It was not quite as ripe as the other she had come across that, judging from the footprints around it, Sumara had encountered. Still, its putrid fragrance was overwhelming. Quickly she continued on her way.

She had not gone far, when Jator's high-pitched laughter reached her ears. Then came his malevolent voice.

"Soon my arrow will sting the life from you, most beloved of sisters!"

The Thorgon girl hurried toward the voice on soundless feet. From somewhere far behind, she heard Korr's voice calling for her and Sumara to come out and leave the king to him. Though she knew his concern for their safety was sincere, it galled her that he evidently placed such little faith in their abilities to deal with Jator. She pressed on; she was too near Jator to give up now. Besides, she would not leave without Sumara.

Reaching a tree, she pressed against its broad trunk and carefully peered at a small clearing a short distance before her. Two empty targets stood on the far side. There was a slight movement in the tall grass on the right side of the clearing. She tensed expectantly.

Then Sumara emerged from the grass and stood hesitantly surveying the area.

Sheela was tempted to call to her, but instinct cautioned her to remain silent. If Jator was indeed lurking nearby, she would give them both away. Bow at the ready, she watched as Sumara cautiously began to skirt the clearing.

Then it happened.

Jator suddenly stepped from behind a target. Drawing his bow, he took aim at Sumara, whose back was to him.

Shouting a warning, Sheela brought her bow up and drew its taut string to its limit. Startled, Jator whirled toward her, while

Sumara threw herself into the tall grass. Sheela loosed her arrow.

The arrow found its mark and tore through Jator's chest, pinning him to the target. His face filled with pain and surprise, Jator stared dumbly at the feathered tip protruding from his chest. Then his body convulsed violently and went limp, hanging impaled on the target, like his many victims.

In her best finery, Sheela stood before Sumara's throne and accepted her friend's praise before a cheering throng of warriors and townspeople. Then she joined Alon, Velor and Zohak on one side of the throne and stood watching while Sumara stood, raised her arms for silence, and announced:

"People of Istwar, I promise to be a fair and just ruler . . . And, with Korr's help, a benevolent queen as well." Smiling, she turned, took Korr's hand in hers, and drew him beside her. "He and I are to be wed this day." Her words met with thunderous approval. She and Korr embraced and kissed, then stood waving to their people as the cheering built to a deafening roar.

That night Sheela slipped away from the celebration and sat in a quiet palace garden. Her task was completed, and Sumara had promised to aid her when she was ready to attempt to free her homeland. Still, she was desolate, wishing that the victory celebration was her own.

"You must not feel sad, my queen," spoke a soothing, familiar voice.

"Tokar . . ." Sheela called, turning and glancing about the moonlit garden. Slowly a wavery form began to materialize before her. Then Tokar's solid, spear-straight figure stood looking down at her.

"You have much to be proud of, my queen. You have united Sumara with her people, and gained a most useful ally for our own people."

"Yet I long for my own triumph . . ."

"It will come . . . in time." Tokar smiled. "Your people keep your memory alive; and the Rhobians still have not subdued the resistance groups that keep our land from their total domination." Sheela beamed, her spirits lifted. Tokar politely cleared his throat and said, "I have again held counsel with Lanzad, who sends you his warmest regards."

"Oh?" Her smile faded and she eyed him dubiously.

The witch-man smiled reassuringly. "Presently, Alon will ask you to accompany him to his homeland . . ."

"And I must accept."

The old man nodded. "For the good of your people."

"So say you and your demon," she said peevishly.

"It will be necessary to have more than one ally, when you finally challenge the Rhobians."

She gave a sigh of resignation and nodded begrudgingly. She was about to speak, when suddenly Alon's voice called to her.

"Farewell, my queen," Tokar said, with a respectful bow. "I will come to you again soon." He quickly vanished like a puff of smoke as Alon's approaching footsteps were heard.

Sheela turned and saw Alon striding up to her. "I have been searching for you," he said eagerly. "There is something most important I must ask . . ."

Smiling brightly, she interrupted him. "I will be happy to accompany you to your homeland, Alon."

For a moment, he was completely taken aback. "How did you know *that* was what I meant to ask?"

"An old man from my country just told me."

Alon cast a glance about the empty garden, then turned back to Sheela, bathed in bright moonlight. He stroked his thin mustache thoughtfully, stared up at the full moon, and nodded. Solemnly he looked down at her and said, "It is not considered wise to sit for too long under the direct light of a full moon."

Smiling inwardly, Sheela stared up at him with large, innocent amber eyes. "It is not?"

"No," Alon replied. He seized her hand, urgently pulled her to her feet, and hurriedly led her toward the palace.

And Sheela was unable to restrain her laughter . . .

Coming in July . . .
Nomad Queen #2:
THE PALACE OF EVIL

Chapter One

The noonday sun was a molten red ball in a colorless sky.

Sweltering beneath their capes, the two riders stoically ignored the scorching rays and pressed their worn mounts ever onward. Aware of the harsh terrain they had to cross, they had been traveling since before dawn's first light, depriving themselves and their steeds of much–needed sleep. Long ago the hard, flat earth had given way to golden sands that swelled into hundreds of smooth, egg-shaped dunes, and beyond brown, bulkless hills, flat against the sky-line, gradually sloped into the rock faces of a formidable yet featureless mountain range. Though the desert ofttimes cruelly jested with the eye, the two estimated they had but less than a half-league's journey before reaching the brown hills. Their path led between twin ridges of dunes and the riders gratefully took advantage of the scant shade.

For hours they had ridden without speaking; the still, hot, dry air and oppressive heat made conversation far too taxing unless there was something of great importance to impart. Now the tall, pale-haired Thorgon girl from the far North Lands broke the silence.

"Is cursed heat all that we may expect from these dismal Southern Lands?" she asked irritably, glowering at the heat waves shimmering across the barren sands. She tossed back her hooded white cape to air her magnificent golden body, nigh-naked save for two sparse strips of soft white leather, with crisscrossing thongs between her firm, bold breasts, and on either side of her smooth, narrow hips. A thin white sword belt accented her slim waist, and her long graceful legs were encased in matching knee-length, snug-fitting, slender-heeled boots. Her only jewelry was a glinting ornate silver necklace.

"Only a true Northlander would find this weather discomforting," said her tall, dark-haired companion, grinning and stretching in his saddle as though invigorated by the arid heat.

Sheela eyed him narrowly, her exquisitely beautiful face clearly expressing her doubt, and shook her flowing mane. She was at least grateful that he no longer referred to her as a Northland barbarian (a most irksome phrase to the proud young Thorgon queen).

"Were we but in the cool, wondrous Northern Lands, I am positive our positions would be the opposite," she said.

"I adapt most easily to any sort of weather," Alon said airily, smoothing his dark, thin mustache. "As a mercenary I have experienced both extremes."

Sheela groaned inwardly and, fearing that he was preparing to once more regale her with yet another tiresome exploit (for Alon's most favored subject was himself), summoned a retort.

But it was never uttered.

The defile unexpectedly opened into a broad sandy waste and they were met by a sight of grisly horror.

It was the place of a recent battle.

Nay, bloody massacre, judging by the profusion of gore-splattered corpses of men and horses strewn about the wide dune-ringed enclosure. The vile stench of death hung trapped in the breezeless air, and violently assailed the nostrils of the living.

Reining in their wheezing, lathered mounts, the man and woman grimly surveyed the silent, butchered mounds and took in yet another horror.

The battlefield was alive with movement.

Hundreds of large, black carrion birds had gathered for a regal feast upon the sorry remains of the once-splendid band of soldiers and nobles who had given their all in an unknown battle. Noisily claiming their territorial boundaries, the vultures, many already too bloated to fly, waddled among the carnage on the blood-drenched sands, plucking sightless eyes from sockets and shredding strips of dead flesh from bones.

Though Sheela was no stranger to a battlefield, the aftermath was still repugnant to her. It was a dreaded reminder of her own frailty. How well one died in battle mattered naught once one was reduced to a lump of putrid flesh, fit only as food for uncaring vultures and other eaters of the dead. Heedless that her worldly companion might regard her actions as womanly squeamishness, she shuddered and turned away.

"Come, let us leave this place," she said solemnly. "There is naught here but death."

"There may be some wretch who still lives," Alon protested.

Sheela's large amber eyes flashed with suspicion. "Do you speak from compassion, or a desire to loot the dead of their belongings?"

"I am no scavenger!" the mercenary replied indignantly. "Oft has a man been left for dead upon the battleground, only to awaken and find vultures tearing at his flesh. I once served with a man who had awoken to find a vulture feasting on his right eye." Despite herself, Sheela grimaced. Encouraged, Alon continued his tale. "He slew the thing too late to recover his eye, and from then on was known as Antar the One-Eye."

"I am sorry I misjudged your intent," Sheela said sincerely, wishing to close the morbid topic. Still, she had no desire to wander among the slaughter in the vain hope that some stranger might have survived.

But then Fate took a hand.

A feeble cry, barely audible above the quarreling carrion birds, hung on the still air. Alon and Sheela's sharp eyes instantly scanned the carnage. Nothing moved.

They strained to hear above the shrill squawking. Then, just as they were about to dismiss it as naught, the cry came once more. A gold-cloaked figure on the outer edge of the butchery stirred and weakly raised a bloody hand. The effort was too great; the hand flopped back onto the sand.

Drawing his sword, Alon shouted a war cry and nudged his horse's flanks. Followed by Sheela, he charged through the carnage, scattering the huge shrieking birds. Those who were reluctant to leave their meals or too gorged to move swiftly were trampled into bloody pulp beneath his horse's hoofs. His slashing sword decapitated another that was too stuffed to soar more than a few yards above the ground. Its hideous, headless bulk thudded to earth and flapped about madly in its death throes, adding its blood to the crimson-stained sand, before expiring atop a corpse's chain-mailed chest.

Reaching the wounded man, Alon leaped from his horse and knelt beside him. The wounded man was in his late middle-years. His aristocratic features and once-resplendent attire immediately marked him as a noble. But he was neither soft nor indolent; otherwise, the horrid wounds that gashed his flesh would have claimed his life before now. The blood that wormed from one corner of his mouth stood in vivid contrast to his facial pallor, which matched his small, pointed gray beard. Still, a spark of vitality shone in his partially glazed blue eyes.

"I thank the gods that I have been able to endure until someone arrived to hear my tale," he said in a parched whisper. His grimace became the semblance of a smile as Sheela joined them with a water bag. "They have also benevolently allowed my last vision to be one of beauty." He nodded graciously to Alon. "I meant no offense to you, young man."

"None taken," Alon said, with an equally courteous nod.

Sheela pulled the stopper and started to raise the bag to his lips, but the dying man shook his head. "You have better need of water than I."

"Nonsense," she said soothingly.

"I fear it will only be wasted on me," he said regretfully, drawing aside his blood-soaked cape to reveal that his other hand, clutching a deep stomach wound, held in his slimy gray-green intestines. "For, as you see, it will only pass directly through me." Sheela involuntarily winced at the sickening sight.

He again covered the wound. "I apologize for your distress, but I wished to impress my point."

"Water will do more harm than good," Alon remarked stoically.

Sheela poured a small handful of luke-warm water, wet her finger tips and gently moistened the older man's lips. Then she allowed the remaining water to trickle through her fingers onto his face.

"The young lady will not be denied her ministrations," the wounded man commented with a grateful smile.

"She possesses an extremely strong-willed temperament," Alon said.

"As befits a queen," Sheela added, her throaty velvet voice as cool as a North Land wind.

"You are a queen?" the nobleman asked, his face aglow.

Sheela nodded and sat back on her heels, proudly drawing her slender torso erect. "I am Queen Sheela of the Thorgons, from the Northern Forest Lands." A flicker of confusion played across the bearded man's face. As with nigh all South Land dwellers, he was clearly unfamiliar with the North Land tribes. Attempting to restore her wounded dignity, she continued. "I am friend and ally of Queen Sumara of Istwar, whom I aided in the re-conquest of her throne from the usurper, Jator."

"Then you, above all, should sympathize with my plight," the older man exclaimed, his quavering voice stronger with excitement, "and that of the royal princess Tira of Padisbek."

"This massacre was the result of her abduction?" Sheela ventured.

"Nay, Your Highness," he corrected, "she is held for ransom in the harem of King Olim of Kasbaku."

Sheela was silent, trying to hide her confusion, for she was as unfamiliar with the peoples and customs of this land as they were of hers.

"I, Prince Nergal, was charged with delivering her ransom of fifty thousand gold coins to Olim at his royal palace in Bokrakand."

"Then this was the work of brigands," Alon interjected, his interest piqued at the mention of such a vast sum.

"The work of a royal brigand—Count Dargo, the consort of Tira's cousin Princess Zaona. The king is gravely ill, and should he die before Tira is ransomed, her cousin would rule until her return." Prince Nergal paused, sucking air between his clenched teeth, as a spasm of pain coursed through his mutilated frame. Alarmed, Sheela looked beseechingly to Alon, who grimly shook his head. It finally passed, yet the man's shuddering head movements evidenced his mighty struggle to cling to life. He continued, his voice now a glottal whisper. "Once upon the throne, the unscrupulous Zaona will do all in her power to retain it. Dargo's actions this day prove her ruthless intent."

"What do you wish of us?" Sheela asked, ignoring Alon's wary sidelong glance.

"Your pledge to recover the stolen ransom and expose Zaona's treachery, thus restoring my lost honor."

"A trifling task," Alon muttered, raising his eyes skyward. Sheela shot him a withering glare.

"Besides myself, both Princess Tira and the people of Padisbek will be in your debt," the prince said, his voice waning.

"You have my royal word," Sheela said in earnest. To her surprise Alon spoke without her urging.

"And mine, too." He grinned and added, "Though it merely be that of a common mercenary."

"That is ofttimes worth far more than one of a common nobleman's," the dying Prince said benignly. He stared up blearily at the two faces above him. "Now I may take my leave of you, and stand before my gods in peace." His head violently jerked, teeth grinding in agony, as he begrudgingly relinquished his grim hold on life. Then the cloud abruptly vanished from his blue eyes and there was a moment of complete lucidity. He gaped in anguish and disbelief at his bloodied form and remarked sadly, "Death is such an unsightly affair. . . ." Long flecks of red spittle spewed from his gasping mouth as his body gave a final forceful shudder and was still. Life fled his body in a protracted sigh that seemed to linger in the still air.

"It is done," Alon said quietly.

Sheela nodded numbly, unable to wrench her eyes from the slack-jawed corpse that stared up at her with glazed blue eyes. She had seen men and women die swiftly in combat, but this lingering death was unsettling. It again pressed home her own vulnerability. She felt Alon's hand on her arm. He was speaking but morbid thoughts deafened her ears to his words.

Suddenly her feral instincts vanquished all thought. She sensed more than heard movement behind her. Then came a thunderous voice:

"Away from him, you damned pillagers of the dead!"

Sheela whirled to see what appeared to be an animated corpse hurtling toward her, his upraised scarlet-tipped sword glistering wickedly in the sunlight. His face was an indistinguishable mask of blood, punctuated only by the whites of his eyes which stood out in horrid contrast. Blood streamed in tiny rivulets down his brawny, gilded-mail chest, and from numerous wounds upon his massive frame. Awestruck, Sheela could but gape in stunned revulsion at the fast-approaching horror.

Then Alon's urgent shove sent her sprawling sideways to land beside the dead nobleman, breaking her semi-mesmerized state. She raised herself up onto an elbow and saw Alon snatch his sword from the ground and spring up to intercept the living corpse.

"Hold, my friend," he shouted, "we are no—"

The big man lunged at him, sword slashing downward. Alon leapt back and whirled his sword up, parrying the mighty blow that was meant to split him from shoulder to groin. The crimson-faced man relentlessly continued his attack.

Steel rang on steel in a deadly flurry of action too swift for the eye to pursue as the combatants, sparks flying like lightning from their blades, gave stroke for stroke. The sharp metallic sounds were exaggerated on the still air as the savage contest raged in and out of the ragged rows of dead. Though taller and heavier than the lean, muscular mercenary, the huge man was fast for his size and, despite his wounds, seemed to possess unflagging vigor. Alon was hard put to avoid his fierce onslaught.

Gaining her feet, Sheela cried, "Do not kill him, Alon!"

"My concern is that he does not kill me!" Alon growled, parrying furiously as he steadily gave ground. Surely it was but a matter of time before his ghastly adversary would succumb to his wounds—but Alon wondered if he would still be alive by then. Blade held in a good defensive position, he continued his weaving, dodging retreat with pantherish grace.

Her lovely face etched with concern, Sheela stood watching and listening to the steady clanging of their blades and the grate of steel gliding off steel as they relentlessly attacked and counter-attacked. She was well aware that Alon's manly pride would not endure her intervention, so there was naught to do but trust in Fate and his skill as a swordsman.

Then it happened.

As Alon nimbly leapt aside from a terrific stroke he stumbled against a corpse and went down flat on his back. He stared up dazedly at the formidable figure looming over him, pale eyes flashing maliciously inside their hideous red mask, massive sword-arm raised to strike.

"*No!*" Sheela shouted urgently, her blade rasping as it flew from its scabbard. She ran forward, aware that there was scant hope of reaching Alon before the murderous blow.

The brawny man froze, sword poised to half Alon in twain. Then, as though buffeted by a mighty, invisible hand, his knees abruptly gave way and, his strength spent, he toppled forward. The mercenary hastily threw himself aside, narrowly avoiding being trapped beneath his massive bulk. The brawny man hit the ground with a jarring, dust-stirring thump.

Alon sat up, coughing and waving aside the settling dust, then glanced over at his fallen adversary, and sighed with relief. Hearing Sheela's anxious voice, he turned to see her approaching and flashed a broad, reassuring grin.

"It appears that I may yet see the sun set this day."

She stopped before him and stood gasping from exertion. "You are unhurt?" she asked.

Alon threw off his cape and stared down at himself. His once loose-fitting, blue-silk shirt was plastered to his sweat-drenched torso; his soft, tawny leather breeches and knee-length boots, emphasizing his sinewy leanness, were spattered dark with blood. He looked up at Sheela and nodded. "But no thanks to our oafish friend here."

Sheela turned her eyes to the fallen man. "He is dead?"

With some effort, Alon heaved the motionless man onto his back and leaned over him. A layer of golden sand partially clung to his blood mask, slightly lessening his grotesque appearance. His mighty chest rose and fell inside its gilded mail. Alon turned back to Sheela and announced, "He lives."

"Then we will tend his wounds."

"We!" Alon exclaimed, his brow furrowed in indignation. "I am not even fond of this fellow."

Sheela gave an uncaring shrug. "Very well, I shall tend him."

Finding himself the object of her large, scornful amber eyes, Alon heaved a resigned sigh. "I will fetch water and bandages. . . ."

After bathing the sand and blood from the big man's face, Sheela was surprised to see that he was a handsome, strong-jawed youth, not more than two summers older than herself. The saber cut above his forehead was less serious than it first appeared, and, with

Alon's begrudging aid, was easily stanched and bandaged with a strip of clean cloth. Likewise, his other wounds were superficial, but the loss of blood had depleted his strength.

"Pray, what are we to do with this 'foundling?'" Alon asked testily, still deep in his sulk.

"Take him to the nearest village," Sheela replied.

"That means traveling several days out of our way," the mercenary protested.

"So be it," Sheela said simply.

"This fellow is a nuisance," Alon grumbled. "You should have allowed me to kill him during our combat." Disregarding her coolly skeptical expression, he continued. "He will wake with a most fierce headache and numerous other pains. It would be a merciful act to see that he does not awaken."

"You would kill the only witness to Count Dargo and Princess Zaona's treachery!" flared Sheela. Alon was taken aback; this was plainly something he had not considered. "None in Padisbek would believe the word of strangers against Zaona." She motioned to the unconscious man. "But he is one of their own."

"Ah, of course," Alon said, nodding at her logic. "This fellow returns to tell his tale,

306

while we continue on to my homeland."

"Have you forgotten our pledge to Prince Nergal?"

Alon shook his head impatiently. "That was before we knew there was a survivor. But now there is no need for us to meddle in the royal affairs of a strange land."

Withering disdain flashing in her eyes, Sheela opened her mouth to unleash a scathing discourse on pride, honor and integrity, but was interrupted by a loud groan. Abandoning her intent, she turned to the wounded man as he awoke with a start, his eyes wide and bewildered.

"You are in no danger," she said, placing a gentle, restraining hand upon his shoulder. A huge hand clumsily caught her slim wrist in a bone-crushing grip.

Instantly Alon's dirk was at the young man's throat, its needle point pressing his jugular. "You are causing the lady pain, my friend," he said, his smile belying his deadly intent. "Now you will remove your hand from her and apologize like a well-bred little gentleman, or I will take great satisfaction in opening your gullet." The youth's pale eyes smoldered resentfully as his thick fingers reluctantly uncoiled from Sheela's bruised wrist. "That's better," Alon said. "Now—"

"Kill me and be done," interrupted the young man defiantly. "But I'll not apologize to a filthy looter!"

"My ill-bred, misguided friend," Alon said in polite rebuke, "this is Queen Sheela from the Northern Lands; and I am Alon the mercenary, late a general in the army of Queen Sumara of Istwar, and we are certainly no looters."

The young man's eyes shifted questioningly to Sheela, who sat rubbing her wrist. She nodded in confirmation and gave him her most haughty, queenly stare. His countenance softening, he said, "I, Prince Bresar, betrothed to become the royal consort of Princess Tira of Padisbek, do offer my sincere apology for my rude actions, Queen Sheela."

"I accept, Prince Bresar," Sheela said graciously. "Now let us think no more about it."

Alon put away his dirk and said dryly, "This seems to be our day for meeting royalty." He grinned down at Bresar. "I am glad I did not have to open your throat; otherwise, our efforts to tend your wounds would have been for naught."

Prince Bresar painfully drew himself to a sitting position and touched his bandaged forehead. "I am grateful for your care." His eyes took in the other bandages on his limbs and torso. "You have done a most admirable task." Grimacing, he rose and swayed unsteadily on his feet.

"You must rest," Sheela said solicitously, placing a steadying arm about his waist.

"I can not tarry any longer," the young man said, regaining his equilibrium and drawing away from her arm. "I must find those responsible for this and recover what has been taken."

"That will be quite a feat for one man without a horse," Alon remarked.

"There are three of us and two horses," Sheela said.

"What!" Alon exclaimed.

"We gave our word," Sheela reminded him pointedly.

"But—" Alon began.

"I know naught about your word," Sheela interrupted, "but my royal word is most precious to me."

"This is sheer madness!"

"You are well aware that I am in these Southern Lands to win allies to my cause of driving the Rhobian conquerors from my homeland."

"You can make allies in my homeland!"

"I hope to. But for now, I am honor bound to aid Princess Tira."

"Then you do so alone!"

"If I must," Sheela said firmly, standing proud and erect. In her high, slender-heeled boots she stood two fingers taller than Alon, who stretched his lean frame in vain as he determinedly met her inexorable gaze.

"That is your final word?" Alon asked, fuming inwardly.

"It is," Sheela replied icily.

"Then I leave you to your folly." Alon gave a curt bow, turned on his heel and strode toward his horse.

"I do not wish to cause trouble between you," Bresar said awkwardly.

"You have naught to do with this," Sheela snapped, her eyes on Alon's straight back. "We gave Prince Nergal our word to recover Princess Tira's ransom and expose Zaona and Count Dargo. And I fully intend to do just that."

"I welcome your aid, Queen Sheela."

Sheela nodded absently, her eyes intent upon Alon's back. She wished to call to him, but her pride would not allow it. They had been through much together since that day he had rescued her from a cave lion in the Land of the Thirsty Death, and she regretted their harsh parting. But a queen must stand by her word regardless of the consequences—especially a queen without a

country—for her word was all she had to live
by.

Alon paused beside his horse and prepared
to mount. He hesitated and cast a glance
back at the young North Land queen. Her
cool amber eyes upon him, she stood arrow
straight, her head held proudly. By all the
gods, whenever she was in one of her righ-
teous moods—which were far too many—she
was oblivious to all else, no matter how logi-
cal the argument. Ofttimes he had sorely
wished to seize her soft, straight shoulders
and shake her 'til she surrendered to reason. And this was one of those times. But
he knew it would accomplish naught, save
to further arouse her barbarian ire. How in
Hades did she and a wounded youth expect
to go against a band of butchers and take
back the ransom—especially without his fine
expertise?

As Alon continued to ruminate he knew
he'd be haunted for the rest of his travels by
the image of the tall Thorgon girl's proud,
slender form, her light hair, burnished gold
in the sunlight. The question of their fates
would long trouble his thoughts.

Curse the gods for this dilemma they had
set upon him! he thought. Fond memories,
some most intimate, raced through his mind.
Damn it all, he had not saved this girl's life

more than once, only to abandon her now to certain death! He gave a deep sigh of resignation and then said, "Well, what are you waiting for? I thought you were in a great haste to right injustice!"

As she hurried toward him, followed by the youthful prince, the Thorgon's queen's radiant smile made Alon feel impervious to the danger that lay ahead.

Well . . . almost.

The malevolent sun was still high in the sky as they emerged from the brown hills and halted before the mountain range. The tracks of the two score horsemen that they had been following since leaving the desert massacre site led up a slender path into the mountains.

"Count Dargo seeks an odd route back to Padisbek," remarked Prince Bresar.

Alon turned in the saddle and looked at the young man riding behind him. "The fools have sealed their doom. The Kobistan mountains are home for over a dozen fierce tribes who live by robbery. Those pampered palace brigands are no match for skilled mountain warriors."

"There is still the matter of the ransom," Sheela reminded him, studying the rugged peaks, rising range upon range into the azure sky. "It matters naught which group has it, we must take it from them."

"That is much easier said than done, my bold-spirited Northlander," Alon said.

"A way will present itself." She quickly nudged her horse forward before he could retort. She had no wish to engage in a foolish argument, for fear that her acute discomfort with great heights would weaken her resolve.

"Curse us for even bigger fools than Dargo and his lot," fumed the mercenary. Muttering an invocation to the mountain people's winged god who watched over robbers, he grudgingly kicked his mount forward, and took over the lead.

They cautiously started up the narrow trail which passed out of sight into a series of sharp bends, and soon crept along the edge of a chasm yawning so close that two sideward paces would prove fatal. The angle of the path became so steep as it continued to dizzily zigzag skyward that they were forced to dismount and, clinging to stirrups, let the horses haul them along.

The next quarter-league was a nightmare. While it was far from disagreeable to be buffeted by winds which were no longer from the hot desert below, the three were still bathed in sweat from their exertion. It stung and blinded their eyes, increasing the danger of a fatal step or stumble. Their lungs labored like a blacksmith's bellows; every bone and muscle ached intolerably. The calves of their legs swelled 'til it seemed they would burst through their encasing boots; scarcely could they place one foot before the other. Bresar's wounds soon leaked beneath their bandages, but he paid no heed. A man can endure much when the fate of his beloved is at stake.

Their progress was slow and most arduous. They would climb a hundred or so paces, halt to rest, and then repeat the process again and again. Finally, when mind and body had reached the limit of their endurance, the trail widened and sloped downward, toward a small, pine-clad valley.

It was then that the sounds of a raging battle reached their ears.

Too winded to speak, the three exchanged knowing glances and, leaving their frothing horses, wearily scrambled up into a group of rocks on one side of the trail. From their vantage point they stared down at a battle without quarter being fought in numerous individual clashes about the sunlit clearing. The complete chaos clearly showed that Count Dargo's black-and-scarlet men had been caught by a surprise ambush. The victors had now become the vanquished. But they, indeed, died hard, fighting with but one intent: to wreak slaughter upon the roughly clad mountain warriors until the end.

As the seething mass of blood-mad tribesmen, their small, shaggy horses dwarfed by the intruders' larger mounts, overwhelmed the valiant band, a rider in total black, upon an equally black horse, won free and raced back toward the trail. Two whooping warriors charged after him. The black horse, laboring and panting hard, was fast tiring, and the pursuers quickly halved the distance between them.

Prince Bresar tensed excitedly. "That's Count Dargo fleeing for his life!"

"To blazes with him," Alon said. "The ransom has now changed hands."

"That does not relieve us of our pledge," Sheela stated, not taking her eyes from the approaching horsemen. Alon sighed his discontent at her words.

As the two tribesmen closed on either side of him, Count Dargo's sword arm moved in a seemingly casual gesture, as though swatting away a pesky insect. Almost simultaneously his two attackers fell from their saddles; one spouting scarlet from a half-severed neck, the other spewing gore from a head neatly divided in twain from crown to chin.

"He may have escaped those savages," Bresar cried, "but he'll not escape me!" He lunged to his feet and ran to the edge of the rocks overlooking the trail. As the black horseman approached, Bresar whipped off his cape and hurled it down.

The fluttering cape enveloped the startled horse's head, bringing it to an abrupt halt. Shrilly whinnying in terror, the animal reared on its hind legs, almost dispelling Dargo from its back, and frantically shook its head, seeking to dislodge the blinding, clinging cloth. Before Dargo could bring his mount under control, Bresar leapt down on top of him.

Together men and screaming horse slammed heavily to the ground in a wild tangle. The stallion struggled to its feet and, free of the cape, bolted down the trail, leaving the men rolling about, locked in fierce combat. Their frenzied conflict took them nearer and nearer the cliff's edge. Grappling, they gained their feet and began pummeling each other.

"They fight more like peasants in a barnyard than royalty," Alon observed.

"I wish Bresar would hurry and dispatch him," Sheela said, prudently dividing her attention between the contest and the clearing, where the battle had ended and looting had now begun.

Bresar caught the black-clad count in a bear-hug and hoisted him off the ground. But before ribs or backbone could be cracked, Dargo smartly slapped his open palms against his opponent's ears, nigh rupturing his eardrums.

Giving an anguished gasp, Bresar hurled the count away, sending him reeling to the edge of the abyss, and clutched at his throbbing ears. Dargo recovered, realized his perilous position and, pulling a knife from his boot, tried to dash past the faltering Prince.

That was his undoing.

With the swift speed of a striking cobra, Bresar's huge hands shot out and closed on Dargo's throat. Arms and legs flailing, the black count was again lifted off his feet. Aware of his waning strength Bresar's fingers squeezed mightily, seeking a quick end to the struggle. The count's coldly handsome face flushed with blood and his discolored tongue protruded between his frothing lips. Truly, the end was near. In a final, desperate effort he plunged the knife downward, into Bresar's shoulder.

Ignoring the pain, the brawny prince staggered to the edge of the trail and, raising

Dargo above his head by his neck, flung the count from him—straight out into thin air.

Clothes billowing in the wind, the madly thrashing black form hung for an instant suspended in space, then, with appalling swiftness, plummeted from sight. The gorge echoed his chilling screams, which became fainter with his rapid descent, until an outcropping rock brought them to an abrupt end.

Bresar stumbled back from the edge and jerked the protruding knife from his shoulder. With that act, his reservoir of strength was depleted and he collapsed unconscious, his head and shoulders dangling over the side of the gaping ravine.

Alon and Sheela scrambled down from the rocks and ran to Bresar. They urgently tugged him away from the edge and struggled to lift him to his feet. It was no easy task.

"Alon, hurry!" Sheela implored.

"This is like trying to heft an ox," he grunted.

Sheela suddenly froze, her head jerking in the direction of the clearing as the drumming of horses' hoofs reached them. Her large amber eyes widening fearfully, she bit her lower lip in an effort to retain her self-control and looked hastily to the mercenary.

"Shall we leave him?" he asked.

She shook her head determinedly and strained harder to raise the unconscious man as the ominous hoofbeats drew nearer. With Alon's aid, Bresar was on his feet and, supporting his dead weight between them, the two laboriously started for the sheltering rocks.

But it was too late.

Around the bend tore six savage warriors, their cloaks of dyed camel hair swirling in the wind. The three were quickly intercepted and driven back toward the yawning chasm. Avoiding the rearing horses, Alon and Sheela retreated with their burden, until they could go no farther. They had reached the mouth of the ravine.

Sheela nervously felt the loose ground crumbling beneath her slender boot heels, but there was no way past the rearing horses' pawing hoofs. In only a matter of seconds she and the two men would be falling backward . . . into eternity.

To be continued. . . . Look for James Gordon White's epic adventure, *Nomad Queen # 2: The Palace of Evil,* on sale in July at newsstands and bookstores everywhere.